P9-DEL-742

THE MAN WHO SNAPPED HIS FINGERS

Fariba Hachtroudi

THE MAN WHO SNAPPED HIS FINGERS

Translated from the French
by Alison Anderson

Europa Editions
214 West 29th Street
New York, N.Y. 10001
www.europaeditions.com
info@europaeditions.com

First Publication 2016 by Europa Editions

Translation by Alison Anderson
Original title: *Le Colonel et l'appât 455*

Library of Congress Cataloging in Publication Data is available
ISBN 978-1-60945-306-0

Hachtroudi, Fariba
The Man Who Snapped His Fingers

Book design and cover illustration by Emanuele Ragnisco
www.mekkanografici.com

Prepress by Grafica Punto Print – Rome

Printed in the USA

To you, my Del

I didn't sleep a wink all night. A sleepless night in a pale, wakeful sleepwalker of a city. The country has been covered in snow for three months. The sun hasn't gone down in four months. It floods the expanse of crystallized ice. Diamonds for cutting throats. I loathe this mass of ice with its blinding clarity, its unhealthy reverberations.

It is six o'clock in the morning. I leave the center and take the train at six-thirty. A heavy mist smothers the desolate horizon of this rotten suburb. A lunar landscape, fraying as far as the capital. The fog calms me, penetrates me, engulfs my being. I become blurred, I merge with my surroundings. This suits me perfectly. I can no longer stand clarity. Precision frightens me. Definite outlines oppress me. I vacillate, stagger. Even when I'm sitting down. It's intoxicating.

The central station is deserted. At eight-thirty I arrive outside the closed doors of the Office for Refugees and Stateless Persons. The building is a fifteen-story skyscraper, a beehive. With hundreds of little offices. The office for asylum seekers and stateless persons is on the sixth floor. The one where I have an appointment is located on the left in a long corridor. I know my way by heart. I could get there with my eyes closed, walking backwards. You go in through a creaking sliding door. There is a Formica table on the right as you come in with three chairs, including the one for the presiding official. The only one with an adjustable back. If I were clever with a pencil, I could draw the dog-eared map that is taped to the wall on one side, the worn-out coatrack, the plastic cups, the half-filled bottle of water, the files—including my own—piled on the table. This office is actually an interrogation room that does not say its name. Prison, cell, cage, solitary, I know all that.

Killing time. Half an hour until the doors open. I'm stamping my feet to keep warm, chanting your name. *Vima, Vima, Vima.* I miss you, Vima. Yes, more than our little Urania. More than our fine son. Not as little as all that, Urania? A regular young lady, you tell me? Sixteen years old, already. And as pretty as a picture? I don't doubt that. But not as pretty as you. She will never be as pretty as you. Sixteen years old! I've been gone for five years? I can hardly believe it. How have I managed. So far from you. From the warmth of your body. I dream of it day and night. Your breasts. Your hips. The small of your back. What did you say? The boy is a full head taller than you! Already a man. Your little man, since my escape? He had better look after you the way I did, better than I did. Otherwise—watch out. Tell me instead about yourself . . . About yourself, my joy and my pain. I miss you more than I miss them. Why shouldn't I say as much? Since it's the truth. I promised you I would never lie again. You remember, don't you? You made me swear on the heads of our children. Lying is our calamity, you said. The country is sick with it. You said, Those damned tricksters with their muddled brains have abused us, they're monsters. And you added, Their deception has turned you into an assassin. Don't you remember? You were right. An assassin . . . In spite of myself. I was a murderer, blessed by the Supreme Commander, and saved by you. It's true. I was like them, for years I lied to you. When you found out that I hadn't really resigned from the Army. That I wasn't really a businessman. That everything was hypocrisy and counter-truths. You exploded. You leave them for good or I'll leave you, you said. You despised me, you were horrified that I was working for the country's prisons, the most terrifying on earth. I tried to explain to you. That I had no choice. That you don't question the orders of the Supreme Commander. That you can't say no to him, ever. It's a lifelong privilege, where your life is at stake. They tell you as much already on the first day. To belong to the faithful, to be admitted among the holy of holies, is a profession of faith. You no longer belong to yourself. That's the ultimate, irreversible prerogative. A commitment you make on your own. What did you expect? That I would unveil the secrets of the Circle? And sign your death warrant at the same time? No, I kept my mouth shut the way I should. I told you, The less you know, the better. Your safety depends on it. Yours, and the children's. And then you looked at that damn CD. And you found out. It changed our life. I begged you to listen to me, in spite of my lies. Or, rather, because of my lies. I begged you to understand me. To give me some time. I told you, I have to make myself scarce if I want to get away from those murderers. I have to go far away. Beyond reach. Otherwise they'll kill me. All the more reason, get out of here right now, you replied. Do you realize, you were telling me to get out. You were driving me away, without a regret. You gave me that dark look, your lips pursed. I had never seen you like that. I would never have dreamt you could be so determined. Leave. Go away. Flee. To freedom. Cleanse yourself of all this filth. And then I'll come and join you . . . Maybe. Otherwise I'll leave you. I don't want my children to have a murderer for a father. Dear lord. You were ditching me. When I think about it. You were threatening a Colonel from the Circle. A guy who could cause both the meek and the mighty to shit in their pants! A high-ranking officer from the Army of the Theological Republic—and you had him on his knees. A member of the Supreme Commander's inner circle.

The Commander with the silver beard, whom I loved like a father, at the beginning of my career. Why did he choose me from among so many others? Why did he take me under his wing? Why did he want me by his side? I'm an ace when it comes to the latest technology and I'm a crack shot. And he is the most despised of men, surrounded by enemies. Tough men, who dream of getting rid of him. He knew this. He could tell. He admitted as much, one week before I ran away. The paranoia of the tyrant? Go figure.

I went to meet him in the little salon where he receives his loyal followers. A great honor. His eyes were shining with a strange fire. His gaze wandered, drifted, and vanished inside him with constant regularity. Never landing anywhere. The gaze of someone who is alienated, a terrible gaze, suddenly gentle in absence. He asked me to come closer, while he combed his beard with an index finger as stiff as a piece of wood. He spoke through his nose, in a scarcely audible whisper, as if he were afraid of indiscreet listeners: As soon as you finish with the prisons I will appoint you head of my personal guard. I was petrified. I would much rather go on slaving away in the country's prisons. But how to admit it? I protested. Vehemently. I stood up to him. It's impossible. I can't accept it, My Lord. I am not worthy of it. I do not have the necessary experience nor the strength of character required by this honor, which I in no way deserve. He smiled. Magnanimous. Asked me if I intended to disobey him. No. Of course not. I stammered, Far be it from me, the thought of such an affront. I begged him not to overestimate me. I preferred to remain one of his humble servants. At a loss for arguments, I began to weep. Sobbing my heart out . . . I was trembling. I was weeping, to hide my panic. To think I had confronted enemy tanks and bombs without flinching. He placed his fingers, curled like hooks, around my head and whispered, You have my absolute trust, my boy. Your tears are an offering I gladly accept. This madman believed I was weeping tears of love. Indeed, who would dare to weep in his presence for any other reason? His claws, screwing my skull on my neck, unscrewing it, bending my neck. I let myself go on his shoulder and burst into sobs. Tears of helplessness. A raging tide of tears, and His Holiness was upset. Now he began to snivel in turn. The madman was consoling me. Caressing my cheek, whispering in my ear, I no longer trust the people around me. You will be my protector.

It beggared belief. Grotesque. He was placing his trust in me. I had the trust of the most powerful man in the country and I was going to run away. To go over to the other side. I was weeping like a mental retard when I could have killed him. Snapped his neck, just like that, in a fraction of a second. If you had been safe, you and the children, I would surely have done just that. I would have been a hero. The savior of the nation. The man who had rid the country of the vile Supreme Commander.

I'm going to let you in on a secret. It was not because of your threats that I ran away. I would never have let you get away with them. You couldn't leave me. I would have killed you first before taking my own life. No, I ran away to hide my weakness from them, my Achilles' heel. Maybe you don't know Achilles? A mate from Russia, a fugitive like me, half hoodlum half poet, told me the story of Achilles. A magnificent story. I'll tell it to you when you come. What was I saying? Yes, my weakness, my absolute love for you was going to destroy us sooner or later. Because of you I was in their sights, already in my early years in the Army, long before my meteoric rise. Our commander in chief, the terror of the subordinate officers, didn't like women who went where they pleased. Women had to stay at home. The wives of his subordinates in particular. A wife who was at university had no business with a guy from the Army. I was the only one who had such a wife. He took every opportunity to jeer at me. This gentleman's lady wife is studying physics, he would say ironically. Madame is a scientist. Yessiree! If she's so clever, why doesn't she go and work at our family firm's Center for Nuclear Research? Why isn't she in the service of the Supreme Commander? That's not her specialization? Oh, yeah, she's into astrophysics. What sort of rubbish is that? The science of galaxies, stars, and all that stuff? Oh, yeah? Maybe she's actually a poet? A subversive? The kind of woman who is cluttering up our prisons? And he began singing, with that leering face of his, *Madame beep beep physics, beep beep madame physics!* Everyone burst out laughing. Me louder than anyone. I was barking. Croaking. What could I do? He had his nose in my glands. Sniffing my sweat. My love was bound to smell of fear. A poisonous odor. My fear for you poisons me. And the bastard could tell. I had to swear on all the saints that if necessary I would kill my wife and my children to safeguard the Theological Republic and the grandeur of our leader, the Supreme Commander, the representative of divine governance. So I swore. So much it was practically an overdose. The poison made me sick. Do you remember that fever that almost killed me? My temperature that wouldn't go down. The doctors couldn't figure out what was wrong. An evil spell has caused this fever, said my poor old mother. You can't make it better with aspirin, only with faith. I prayed, prayed, and prayed, swearing I would never lie again. Never again would I lynch you on the altar of the Book. I was caught in a vise. You could tell, too, that disaster was imminent. You'd been badgering me for years. It was all you ever said. Resign. Over and over, Resign, relentlessly. Resign, leave the Army. It was your refrain, you served it up at breakfast, at dinner, in bed. Even when I was making love to you. And then one fine morning they offered me a new position in the High Security section. Which would require a radical change of status, said the Commander's envoy. It's the Commander who nominated you, but it's top secret. Which means it calls for anonymity. I would have to resign from the Army. Unofficially, of course, the emissary reassured me. We have to make the country secure, beginning with the prisons, he said. My job would be to determine our needs in sophisticated, high-performance, reliable matériel, then acquire it and oversee the installation. A purely technical job. I would swap my cap and my military uniform for the sort of business suit the CEO of an import-export company would wear. A cover, and a dream opportunity to satisfy you, with an easy conscience. You've been hiding behind your little finger, is what you said, when you saw through the trick. Yes. For lack of choice. Yet again. I might not believe in a miracle, but I thought at least in the meanwhile I would have a reprieve . . . I will never forget your childish joy when I told you the good news. It was a time when quite a few military men were getting involved in business. Retired, disabled men, avid or disappointed soldiers . . . Like everything else, the businesses run by former soldiers were under state control. The Commander's inner circle granted preferential treatment. But you were unaware of such details, my poor love. You weren't interested. You trusted me. You took my word for it when I explained that my partner was a former officer, now retired, who had the capital required to start the business.

You were thrilled at the thought that from then on you'd be seeing me in a business suit and not a uniform. You were happy. I was over the moon. I wore the suits you picked out for me when I visited prisons in the country to determine our requirements in matériel. And the fact those prisons were filled to overflowing had nothing to do with me. The prisoners' conditions under detention were not my problem. Nor was the fate meted out to the politicals, who were systematically tortured behind closed doors in the maximum-security sections. I don't believe I was a coward or a bastard. Merely powerless. But I respected the limits I had set myself ever since I came back from the front. I was a soldier, a military man, and that was what I would remain. I don't get my hands dirty. I don't kill. I don't torture. I never hurt a flea, and I never would. And I keep my word. That is not the case with the careerists who make the rules nowadays. Insipid little guys who've come back from the front and who've made their careers and filled their bank accounts by agreeing to do away not with the enemy on the battlefield but with our own children in the streets of the capital.

Not I. That's what I told myself deep within. And I confess I was pretty proud of myself, until you messed everything up. In short, it wasn't your threats that made me decide to run away and leave everything behind. It was the Commander, and my imminent appointment as head of his personal bodyguards. I would be forced to flee or forced into a corner. The crap businessman would have to change his clothes and proudly display his military stripes. No more putting on acts. I was playing with fire. My terror at being unmasked, by you or someone else, was poisoning my life. In either case your safety would be compromised. You were quicker than them. There was nothing surprising about that. You are a thousand times more intelligent. But I helped you to go about it. I may have been a straw man sort of businessman, an actual agent for Security and Intelligence in the service of the country's prisons, but that straw man had had enough of the national sport, the art of dissimulation the leaders are so good at.

Then the tsunami. A bit sooner than I had planned. 455 was the one who brought it on. You ordered me to leave you and go abroad, and you knew nothing about the Commander's proposal. I obeyed. To keep you out of danger, my love. In those days, I didn't care what happened to 455. In those days, I wasn't thinking of redeeming myself. It was you who wanted it for me. But now I tell myself I can look you in the eyes again with my head held high. Ever since I arrived in this fucking country I haven't lied a single time. Not just to honor my promise. I thought, foolishly, that I could get by without lying. I told myself, You're in a free country. No need to wheel and deal to get by. No need to tell fibs. To embroider my life and deceive others, to lead people up the garden path. I told myself, If you tell the truth about all the shit things that have been done by you and by your superiors, you'll earn if not their respect then at least a chance to benefit from their bullshit human rights. Yeah, right. Five years they've been stringing me along. Five years of asking me the same old questions. Five years they've been recording, copying, recopying the same answers. Then they start again. Over and over. They never get tired. There is always some point that needs clarifying. Some missing element. They have nothing better to do. Yuri was right. He told me that lies make the world go round. And have done so since the dawn of time. There's no reason for anything to change. He said, It would have been better if you'd stayed the schizo you were, rather than become the dumbass you are now. And you'll remain a dumbass as long as you cling to your worthless ideas. He said, The world is amoral. There is no truth or justice. There are only transactions and compromises that are more or less ingenious, more or less unfair. Secret deals that suddenly become plain to see. It's like the story of the clown with his big red nose who wants to play the lion tamer. You get me? I said yes. But I have my own opinion on the matter. Every time I ask him if he's lying when he claims he's being persecuted by Putin, he dodges the issue. I insisted, Were you really an advisor to that billionaire who's in prison? He burst out laughing. The only explanation I got was his same old theory about people being different. Poets are the rare schizos who can do without truth as easily as they can do without lies, he said. They make up stories, they transgress, they know how to change, save the world from its misery, from lies, they are the mirror of the truth. But am I an authentic poet? *That's the question!* The only question worth asking, you great dumbass! I might as well confess I never really know when Yuri is lying. But I take everything he says at face value.

So I stamp my feet out here and I dream. I chant your name. My talisman. Who knows. Perhaps they've summoned me here to tell me it's all over. No more questions. No more points to be clarified. No more doubts about me. Tell me there will be no more sordid detention centers for asylum seekers. No more temporary beds. No more no-man's-lands where people vilify my existence. No more subhuman status. No more temporary papers. Maybe they're going to tell me that at last I have the right to real documents that will allow me to work. To bring you over here. You'll have no trouble finding a position that's worthy of you. You're so good at what you do. They'll be blown away. You'll be a star . . . I can see you running one of their research centers. I stamp my feet and daydream. Fantasies. You in my bed and me inside you. In a little while, maybe I'll hear the magic words: Mr. 43221, your file is closed. Your case has been settled. The authorities, and God the father along with them, believe you. The appellate judge has handed down his decision: accepted! You have the right to become a citizen. The right to our documents. To our freedom. To our security. The right to live without trickery, without nightmares, terror, or the obligation to flatter anyone. The right to give the finger to the Supreme Commander, to forget him, to loathe him along with everything else. For you it's the light at the end of the tunnel.

Turn around. Go back the way you came. Go home. Get into bed and forget him. Let him go. He can manage without a translator. I say these mantras over and over to myself when I see him outside the door to the Office for Refugees and Stateless Persons. But I keep on going. I get closer to the tall building but I don't stop. I don't hurry but I've come inexorably closer. I put one foot behind the other. Why? Why are my legs working independently of my will?

Yesterday I got a call from the Office. They needed a certified translator to fill in. It was urgent, said the metallic voice on the other end of the line. One last interview with an asylum seeker who's a bit of a problem, said my interlocutor, who was not anyone I knew. I thought, he's filling in, too. He went on, It's a colonel from the Theological Republic. But— He interrupted me, I read your file. "Refuses to do any simultaneous translation for military or government personnel from her country of origin." There was a silence. It lasted a few seconds. The man went on, We'll pay you extra, double the usual amount, if you agree. Another silence. He repeated, it's urgent. Well? I should have said no. But then I should not have hesitated for a second. No. *A firm, sharp* no, *without prevaricating. The word no longer belongs—or shouldn't belong—to my vocabulary, even if* Yes *hasn't quite triumphed altogether. The word* no, *flying the colors of captivity, has all the connotations of a prison ordeal. To be avoided. Or, to be used in homeopathic doses. According to my shrink. Consequently, the word* yes *should automatically become one of those hymns to the glory of life which I so sorely need. Another one of the same shrink's ideas; it seemed so stupid at first. And yet the exercise has turned out to be good for me. If I stop saying no, I no longer feel like I'm being attacked. But in this particular case I should have said no. It was a slip of the tongue. I said yes. Without knowing how or why. An unthinkable verbal slip of the most disciplined muscle in my ravaged body. Ordinarily I count to ten before I open my mouth. A lesson I learned from my dear departed grandmother, and which I practiced assiduously in the Supreme Commander's jails. A lesson for life, basically. And which yesterday morning I forgot. To my great astonishment. I still wonder if it was really me who uttered that distinct, curt and unhesitant* yes. *I heard it without recognizing my own voice. It was like some robot, programmed in advance. By whom? To what aim? No idea. And here we go again. Now I can feel my legs urging me on, drawing me toward that tall man who's hopping up and down to keep warm. He's the soldier I'm supposed to help. I'm sure of it. Without a doubt.*

I'm a few feet away from him. He's at least two heads taller than I am. I hurry my step. Go past him. I can hear him mutter a timid good morning. I nod my head, press my lips, and punch in the code to unlock the green button for the employee interphone. I ring the bell, again punch in the numbers and letters of my ID, the magic formula which gives me access to this sanctuary of hope, "to the possibility of being." A free individual in a society governed by the rule of law. The doors creak. I enter the building and hurry to the elevator. Sixth floor, Room 2304. Here I am. The man in charge, the department head—among colleagues they call him the big boss—greets me. He is visibly surprised. He refrains from asking any questions. This is indeed the first time I've agreed to an interview with an official from my country of origin, a military man on top of it. I have a quarter of an hour before I will find myself in the presence of the man I saw outside the entrance. A brute. With a massive, imposing build. Having said that, if he had been a puny little one-eyed hunchback he still would have been a barbarian. Just like the other mercenaries from a regime that tortures, terrorizes, and oppresses my compatriots, holding them hostage in their own country. I have fifteen minutes to change my mind. Fifteen minutes, or nine hundred seconds. Which is plenty of time to get out of it. I can pretend I don't feel well, come up with a pretext, some emergency, some sudden family matter . . . I can't make up my mind. I'm trying to think. In vain. My thoughts drift, and come apart as soon as they occur to me. I'm passive. I stare at the screen on my laptop, and count the passing minutes. Suddenly it comes to me in a flash. Why should I run away? If anything, this is a bad day for the big man downstairs. The presence of the big boss is not a good sign. He is the last one who questions the asylum seekers before they close the case for good. In 99.99% of the cases the request is rejected. The thought is comforting. Enchanting. I'll stay. I'll do whatever it takes to eradicate the Colonel from the list of candidates for human dignity. You can count on my overzealousness, you son of a bitch.

The boss is speaking to me. Pardon? He says, Would you like to take a look at the questionnaires which I have . . . No. He is surprised. He knows me well enough to be astonished by such abrupt verbal velocity. There's nothing impulsive about me. I don't like negatives. I don't seek out the word no *and I have made this widely known. I've been working here for three years, and no one has ever heard me utter a categorical* no. *They call me Mrs. Maybe, Miss Why-Not, the we'll-see girl . . . These nicknames for the interpreter with the Olympian calm suited me fine. I was proud of them. Until today. The arrival of the soldier, visibly, has changed things. The word* no *has invaded my repertory. The big boss asks me if everything is all right. I look at him, vacantly. He rephrases his question, he can't help it, it goes with the job. As if I were one of those unfortunate fugitives who want to trick him so he has to trap them. Madame, is there a problem? I take a deep breath, and count to ten. I am thinking, Absolutely not. But I answer yes, unintentionally. Without batting an eyelash. This yes was not what I was thinking. This yes slipped out—the way the no did, earlier—and it frightens me. I hear it, once again, and don't recognize my own voice. Like yesterday, when I agreed to come. I'm disconcerted. But my traitor of a voice—how phony can you get?—repeats the word* yes, *and follows with, I'm just a bit worried about my son. He's sick. The boss didn't even know I had a son. Nor did I, I feel like saying. And I feel like explaining what it's like, to have a miscarriage in a prison cell. Solitary 32, Section 209 of Heaven Prison. But my voice fell silent. Fortunately. Silence at last, I think, how can you call a prison Heaven? You can never know what's going on in the depths of the Theological Republic. You have to be locked up in there. Let the place penetrate you to the bone. But I digress. Heaven doesn't mean a thing in my mother tongue. The cynicism of wordplay would surely enchant the jailers of the Theological Republic and the Supreme Commander. I'm sorry about your son, I hope it's not too serious, says the boss, dubiously. I don't answer. A self-imposed silence. A storm in my heart. Heaven! The Heaven prison, the programmed rapes. The uninterrupted beatings. Raining down from everywhere. Heaven and its incomparable torturers. Infanticides. The loss of my love child. It was surely for the best. In the order of things. The implacable logic of the footnotes of history. My own history. I probably wouldn't have known how to love that child after Heaven. In the end I say, In fact, he's my nephew. I love him like a son. My voice rescues me with this new lie. The big boss knows I don't have any children, even if he doesn't know that I cannot have any, anymore. I understand, he says, sympathetically. It's time. Are you ready? Good. I'll bring him in. Above all, don't forget that the only purpose of the interview is to verify the Colonel's prior declarations. To uncover any contradictory statements. I think, Count on me to nail that son of a whore. I nod my head.*

What can he possibly know, that representative of the

Universal Declaration of Human Rights, about the contradictions in the twisted minds of the Inquisition? Without me—nothing.

The floor gives way beneath me. I stop on the threshold of the tiny room and gasp. My usual translator is not there. The lady professor of Asian languages from the University, the genteel pensioner, is not there. The little woman with her singsong, peaceable accent, her salt-and-pepper hair, her kindly smile. She is empathetic. She understands fugitives. Feels for them. Doesn't judge them. All she does is translate their pain. I used to find her odd, even suspect. In her book, survivors are always victims. Without distinction, she explained one day, with the same kindly smile and tender gaze which I no longer found suspect. She thinks the way you do, my dear Vima. She thinks I'm a victim. She is a balm for my aching soul. The woman who is now sitting in her place—455—cannot, will not take me for a victim. I look at her and try not to falter. Not to keel over. Not to faint. It was 455 I just ran into outside the building. But I didn't recognize her then. Which is not surprising. She was in disguise. Her hat pulled down over her eyebrows, a scarf over her mouth. Dark glasses. In a way she has always been in disguise. Who could fail to believe in the Almighty's bad jokes now? You used to say, with a laugh, that God plays his best tricks without warning, to punish us. You who never believed in the God of other people any more than you believed in mine. Nowadays I believe in your God. It is your God, the god of numbers and probabilities, who is making fun of me. Yes, there is nothing surprising about the fact that I am now face-to-face with this woman. The woman sitting next to the official, strung as tight as a bow, is none other than 455. The legend of section 209 at Heaven. She is replacing my kind translator, the professor of Asian languages. Can you believe it? She was the *pasionaria* of Heaven, as wild about her husband as I am about you. The innocent woman. A martyr of the resistance who was never sanctified. She should have died. It is to you that she owes her life. Yes, she always wore a good disguise. For me, at any rate. Like all the female prisoners. Her face hidden beneath a hood or a burlap bag. But I also saw 455 without her hood, blindfolded, in the torture chamber. A human wreck, flat on her face after the beating. Her torturers were relentless. She seems to be in fine shape now. Sitting only a few feet away from me, motionless. I'm freezing, but my guts are on fire. A desire to throw up, my guts burning with acid. Do your god's sarcastic remarks make any sense to you, dear Vima? You keep up with what goes on in the skies—can you figure out this message from the Creator? Whether it's my Creator or yours?

Here in this room, Prisoner 455 from Heaven is no longer in disguise. I'm the one who is, with my face plain to see. I can overcome my confusion, elude my memories, defuse the shock. I step forward, confidently. I was properly raised. I know how to control myself. And I have one advantage over her. She doesn't know me.

She is sitting to the right of the head interviewer. A little ways behind them. I am facing them. As usual. In the dock, in a way. The headman looks me up and down. The translator pays me no attention. Her eyelids are lowered, her sidelong gaze is aimed at my legs, or the floor. I can sense her hatred. The way my superior could smell the fear rising off of me.

The headman's pale eyes drill into my pupils. He has placed his broad hands, as white as a corpse, flat on my file—a big binder with several cardboard volumes, the red ones on the top of the pile—and he says, you understand our language fairly well, but you don't speak it. Isn't that right? I don't reply. I nod. He continues, We are going to begin, if you have no objection. Again I nod. We are going to go through your statements point by point. I hold his gaze. Is he capable of reading my thoughts? Do I have any choice, Mr. Fucking Stupid Human Rights? If only I could spit in his face. He smiles, and says, My colleague will motion to you with her hand when you have to stop. I stare at him. Without blinking. Something that makes people uneasy. I know from experience. He remains unruffled. Not the least bit impressed. I don't like the looks of this guy. Maybe he's new. In any case I've never seen him before. Maybe he's a cop. Probably, surely. Yes, without a doubt. There's nothing of the petty civil servant about him. Unthinkable. We live in a democracy, Colonel, and not a tyrannical regime, my lawyer would say. He can be incredibly extravagant, that gentleman lawyer of mine. I don't know if he's pretending or if he really believes the fairy tales he tells me. Someday I'll tell him as much. For me it's definite. That guy reeks of the fuzz. I have a nose for these things. Years of experience. The headman presses his point, indicates a pause is necessary so she'll have time to translate my declarations as we go along.

I'm tense. My back is stiff. My neck is aching. Temples pounding. I'm sweating. A tension that reminds me of Heaven. And my worst memories. I feel trapped. Caught in a snare. The director is going to realize. I'm going to lose my grip and my job along with it. Why the devil did I agree to fill in on this assignment? Stop. Get on with it. Think. I'm garbling my words. Repeating them over and over. I hang on, ingurgitate, steep myself in words, syllable after syllable, until they become meaningless. I'm shooting up on onomatopoeic phrases, about to overdose. Have to go on. Have to hold up. Finish the job. Right to the end. Don't look at him. Above all. Control your voice. Don't betray yourself. The mental training of a former jailbird. It works every time. I feel calm again. I tell myself he doesn't know we're from the same wretched country. And he won't suspect it if I avoid looking at him. People think I'm Mediterranean—Italian, Greek, Spanish. They often tell me that. And the accent from my native region, at the edge of the country, confuses my compatriots. They take me for a foreigner who has a marvelous mastery of their beloved language. I'll stick it out. Whatever the cost. That son of a bitch won't unnerve me. He might even contribute to my healing. If healing is not just an illusion. I have to put the past behind me. My shrink tells me as much, at length, at every session. No, he doesn't say put it behind me but rather deal with it, confront it. Yes, he tells me I have to confront my past. Well, there you are, dear shrink, my past is staring me in the face. Calmly. As if it were nothing at all. There it is, my past. I'm about to start chatting with one of those men who destroyed my life. One of those bastards who killed the child I was carrying. He's there before me. We'll see if I have the nerves to deal with my past. I'm listening, says the director.

He's listening to me. The cop is listening to me. No doubt about it, he's a specialized agent. I don't take my eyes off him. The woman translates. Her eyes down. Maybe she can't look people in the eye. She'll be wearing the blindfold of the political prisoner for the rest of her life. It's depressing. I feel defeated, exasperated. So it will never end. The past will adhere to me. I have no right to a future. This woman's presence is the best proof of that. There's no such thing as coincidence. It doesn't exist. I ask the guy, Where should I begin? Tell me, rather, what you want to hear, that would be easier.

The Colonel is starting to get annoyed. Already with the first questions. His voice is trembling. He's already told his story a hundred times. His work. The reasons for his escape. The itinerary of his escape. How he spent his time the week before his escape. His— The boss interrupts him. He says he may have already told them all that but he has to start over. From the beginning. He is there to verify the contents of his deposition. It's procedure. He has to repeat one more time what he has already said a hundred times. He speaks calmly, slowly, distinctly. I translate.

I stare at the Colonel's knees. They are quivering imperceptibly. The left knee is actually trembling. He grabs his knees with his scarlet hands, which are swollen at the joints. He has pudgy fingers. Gnarled knuckles. His broad hands with their cracked skin calm his knees. The trembling stops. His fingers relax. The Colonel crosses his legs and shoves his hands into his pockets. Please proceed, says the boss.

I went to the front at the age of seventeen. The war had just broken out. I was a volunteer like hundreds of other guys from our village. My brother was at the head of a regiment of the Army of the Lord. That was how we had to refer to the Theological Republic's brand-new army. We were all proud to be soldiers for the Supreme Commander, the new leader. The country had just been attacked by our heathen neighbor. We were defending our fatherland and the new regime which the Lord had blessed. We believed in it. I fought like a dog. Like my brother, who was my model. Like my cousins and thousands of others, while the country burned. We had faith in our superiors in those days. The faith of dogs, who had volunteered for martyrdom—that was our only fuel. Cold, hunger, a lack of ammunition, of sleep, of human warmth: nothing discouraged us. I picked up five medals for heroism, after one year of combat under conditions you simply cannot imagine. With a handful of other young guys, as crazy as I was, we liberated several villages the enemy had invaded. I was their leader. I was all of seventeen, commanding a regiment of rookie soldiers in rags. Scarecrows as stubborn as we were. Peasants, workers, farmers, all followed us, armed with hunting rifles or their bare hands. The dirty war went on for years. But in the end we got rid of the enemy. At the cost of huge sacrifices. While the rich kids in the capital were fleeing the country to avoid their military service, tramps like us were having their brains blown out. I would not disown those years of brotherly abnegation for anything on earth. Do you hear me? Not for anything on earth. Things went downhill after that. I have to agree. But I'll say it again, because you like to hear me repeat my life story, I am proud of the years I spent fighting.

I returned from the front as an officer, ahead of my time because of my exemplary conduct during the holy defense decreed by the Commander, and I was taken on in an elite corps of the territorial Army. I rose rapidly through the ranks. I was good with weapons, and specialized in engines of war and the latest technology. During a competition I was noticed. It was fairly sophisticated equipment, I'll warrant you that. I obtained the first prize and, the following year, a prize for excellence. Since you want me to repeat it to you, I will confirm that I can dismantle all sorts of automatic weapons with my eyes closed, as well as all any number of robots and control and espionage gadgets. Two months after the second competition, I was hired as a trainer for section K in the Army, a sort of holy of holies directly connected not to the staff but to the Residence of the Supreme Commander, head of the armed forces. When was that? You know very well, it's written in black and white in the files piled up there in front of you. In the year 2000. Who was I training? As you already know, it's in the signed deposition, and I've already told you a hundred times. Officers from our regiments and foreign volunteers. From fraternal countries. What's that? Yes, they were volunteers, destined for outside operations. I beg your pardon? How do you want me to refer to them? I'm trying to be precise. That's all your colleagues ever say. Be precise. Back there, these candidates were destined for martyrdom, they were our brothers in arms, valiant combatants in the service of God. They came from neighboring countries but also from Africa. There were a few Westerners, too. Quite a few, actually. The leaders pampered these neophyte apprentices. We were told they were going to help their countries cast off the yoke of heresy and decadence. Having said that, if you prefer I can use your regulation terminology—they were terrorists, jihadists, converted crusaders or . . . Shall I go on? Can we move on to other matters?

My promotions! The first one was in the winter of 2003, when the Supreme Commander made a surprise visit to our base. He noticed me and hired me on the spot. I was transferred to one of the top secret services in the Army. Top-level Security. In other words, the Gordian knot of Intelligence, under the control of the Supreme Commander, the most powerful, most feared person in the country. Since 2005, thirty thousand people, directly in the service of the Commander's Residence, have been governing every authority in the country and the eighty million souls under its rule. Yes, my life was turned upside down that day. I thought the day was blessed. In fact it was the most accursed day of my life. To be in the service of the Supreme Commander means completely putting your past behind you. Your identity. Your feelings. Your beliefs. To be in the service of the Supreme Commander you have to accept graciously that your duties are the only rights you can claim as your own. The first duty, a sacred one, is absolute obedience to the absolute Master. The relation of cause and effect is clearly established from day one. Those who work at the Residence go behind the mirror the moment they cross the threshold into that nest of vipers. Any individual incorporated into the Commander's inner circle is no longer his own person. We were subjected to the regime of the Three Fs+S. *S* for self-sacrifice when the commander required it, and the three *F*s were, in order of importance, absolute faith, absolute fidelity, and absolute falsification. Faith and fidelity toward the Circle and those who were close to the Commander. Falsification where everyone else was concerned, the outsiders. Everyone else we were supposed to control, beyond the walls of our forbidden city. I would learn to lead a secret life in the bosom of my own family. What would you call this? Schizophrenia? Multiple personality disorder?

For a fraction of a second I can see Yuri in the place of the guy giving me the third degree. I'm thinking, Filthy cop, but I say I don't really understand these scholarly words. I add that I went along with it all the best I could. My life was unfolding in a closed circuit. I would change my identity the way I changed my shirt. As far as my family was concerned, I was a businessman. It was the explanation for my sudden fortune, it justified the extravagant salary deposited every month into the account of the director—who happened to be me—of a front that belonged to the Circle. I moved into a magnificent house, with garden, swimming pool, and all the trimmings. I lived like a prince. But in a permanent state of anxiety. The Residence was worse than the Army. Any discussion outside the order of the day was off-topic. Questions were forbidden, dangerous. We all tried to outdo each other when it came to showing our loyalty to the Commander. It was a contest in obsequiousness. We reveled in our degradation. But I didn't want to get my hands dirty . . . I beg your pardon? You want me to repeat that? I told you I didn't want to get my hands dirty. That's right, sir. You want me to explain? And yet it's simple, I never killed anyone. Never, do you hear me? Except as a soldier in the field of battle. You're at liberty not to believe me. What did you say? I was training others to kill? Not at all, sir. I was training people how to use combat matériel and cutting-edge technology. Those were my fields of expertise. You want me to remind you whom I was training? You want to know whether the volunteers from other countries were potential suicide bombers? The kind who blow themselves up on buses and subways and kill innocent people? Could be. To be exact, I would even say definitely! Are you satisfied? But it wasn't my remit to keep up with what those guys got up to once their training was over. No, that wasn't my problem. It was their problem and that of their hierarchical superiors in the operational sector. It wasn't my signature authorizing their missions. What? What do you mean afterwards? What was my remit? You have it in the miles of paperwork there before your eyes.

Twice I was put in charge of the so-called sensitive personnel. In other words: I trained the personal guards for the Supreme Commander's inner circle. Then I joined the exclusive committee of the Commander's personal representatives. In charge of security in penal institutions. It was my job to renovate and oversee the technological installations. As the Commander's representative I automatically became the coordinator between Military Security and Intelligence. In fact, the Commander wanted to clean up both of those mammoth administrations before absorbing them into the top-level sector at the Residence. My role would be to oversee the drastic purges within these organisms. This decision was a consequence of the growing number of spectacular escapes by political prisoners who were considered a risk to the system. There was a scandal when a former highly placed official, now disgraced, escaped from Heaven. In broad daylight. It triggered a crisis among the country's leaders. Because an escape necessarily implies complicity among the personnel. At the top of the ladder, it goes without saying. In other words, those who have the right keys. The prisons of the Theological Republic, reputed to be the best-protected places on earth, had become regular sieves. My job consisted in beefing up the security of the installations. Padlocking the bastions of power. Making them impregnable, the way they'd been in the past. The way they should be. The technical aspect was child's play. Unmasking the traitors, the scum who were responsible, that was another story. I could turn a blind eye to the trafficking, which the guards organized, of drugs, medications, books, or pencils, why not. But to allow the escape of traitors or political prisoners who were viewed as terrorists—never again.

My brain is overheating. I translate the Colonel's words with sickly slowness. My tongue is furred, my mouth is dry. I had him repeat the last sentences, wondering how I myself got out of there.

Who helped me escape from Heaven, since no one paid for my escape? No one had the means to pay for my freedom. Who had the right key to let me run away? How did they get it? To whom do I owe my life? Who is the man my mother qualified as providential? Where is he today? Questions I had pushed aside, had tried to forget. In order to have a life again. And now they are pouring down on me, assailing me. Oppressing me. I should never have agreed to take this assignment. I'm not going to manage. It fills me with fear. The fear of losing my job. The Colonel repeats, It requires astuteness to unmask the high-ranking officials involved.

Astuteness, or even genius. Prisoners and jailers, from the guard to the warden by way of the judges and lawyers in the pay of the powerful, I had my eyes on all of them. Advanced technology is infallible, and in my domain I'm unbeatable. I assured the Commander that very soon everything would be back to normal.

I set up what was needed, where it was needed, to spy on prisoners, jailers, wardens, judges, and court-appointed lawyers. I wove my web. A network of opaque waves, which made them—individually and all together—audible and visible at all times. No one could escape my vigilance. Every one of them, from the greatest to the most insignificant, was under surveillance. Day and night. At work. At home with their families. At home in their beds. Whether they were sleeping or fucking. Visiting family or friends. When they were traveling. By car. By train. By plane. On camelback. Wherever they were, they were under my control. After a few months had gone by, over one thousand seven hundred people had fallen into my net. Guards, wardens, judges, torturers . . . From north to south, from all over the country, by way of the capital, the arrests were multiplying in number.

That was my last position. I had decided it would be the last. Even though the job allowed me to travel. As a businessman, I went around the world. Russia, Japan, Korea, China . . . Beautiful countries. Unforgettable scenery. Fascinating discoveries. I was amazed by the incredible variety of cutting-edge items. The latest in espionage equipment. Miniature devices . . . What did you say? I don't understand. What do you mean by instruments of a particular kind? The ones used for brutal interrogations? Do you mean instruments of torture? I swear, you are obsessed! I already answered this question. In the first place, it wasn't my sector. In the second place, we didn't need to go abroad to get devices like that. Our correspondents delivered them to us. Russians, Chinese, Koreans . . . Consultants who were officially appointed by their respective governments. There were also the unofficial consultants. Arms dealers are increasingly trading in interrogation technology software. Something of a cynical pun, I agree. But significant. And I'm not the one who invented the term. I am only using it in an attempt to be precise. Software means maximum efficiency without any drawbacks. No collateral damage. Not a trace on the body.

I'm suffocating. I don't feel well. I can't breathe. I am dying to grab him by the throat. The bastard, the way he articulates the words sophisticated software, *so self-assured . . . I see myself back in solitary. My mouth forced wide open, in a jaw-crushing grip. My mouth is a toilet bowl. For the requirements of the penis pissing between my teeth . . . I don't need software to slaughter you without leaving a trace, you monster. I stop the screams coming from deep inside, filling my lungs to bursting. I clear my throat, to rid it of the aftertaste of this traceless torture. All I do is translate. Tell us about these foreign consultants, asks the boss, calmly.*

Consultants? Oh, yes, the Russians. A whole load of Russian officers. They gave classes and trained the local interrogators. Or the torturers, if you prefer the exact terminology. It's the truth. They were torturers. Obviously, I had to know about it. But no more than that. I didn't have anything to do with the dirty work. No, I wasn't present at the interrogations. I did, however, occasionally see video recordings of some of them. The brutal ones, as you call them. There had to be verification, in the event there was cause to suspect any complicity between prisoners and authorities. When my subordinates couldn't cope, I would intervene. It was up to me, in the end, to decide one way or the other. Why did I run away? But how many times do I have to tell you? I didn't want to become the Supreme Commander's plaything. He wanted me for a guard dog. I would have to be at the Residence. Live there three hundred and sixty-five days a year. And if I refused, I was a dead man. That makes sense, doesn't it?

Why did he refuse? Was he suddenly feeling remorse? I translate the boss's questions, articulating each word to modulate my voice, to keep it calm and neutral. The Colonel doesn't reply. He's unnerved. I can tell from the way his knees are trembling, more than ever. He stands up. All of a sudden. He needs to go to the toilet. He has to take some medication. He has a stomach ulcer, and heart palpitations. An irregular heartbeat, he says. His staccato voice slips, falters when he says irregular heartbeat. Is he hoping to make us feel sorry for him? Well, I won't. Let the bastard die. I won't lift a little finger. If I could look at him. Flood him with my hatred. Bury him alive. I keep my eyes down. Obstinately. My gaze slides from his knees to his feet. A giant's feet, in military boots. Eloquent feet. They step forward and head toward the way out. I stifle the cry in my throat with a cough. The Colonel isn't wearing military boots, he's wearing sneakers. I immediately understand why I was mistaken. It's his walk that led me astray, blurring my vision. A walk like a lame duck, with his right foot turned inwards. It blurred not my vision but my perception. I saw a memory, or thought I did. It's always like that, when buried images take the place of reality. I'm frozen stiff. All of a sudden. The snapshots from Heaven prison stored on the hard drive in my brain are emerging, out of order, in slow motion. Do I recognize the Colonel's feet? Those big feet, with their awkward movement, remind me of the feet of the man who burst into the interrogation room. I was close to death. They told me my end was approaching. My imminent execution. They were going to send me to the gallows . . . I have to get a grip on myself. I must be hallucinating. Haunted by the memory of a twisted walk. Of a pair of giant's feet. Feet, and the way they walk, flimsy clues political prisoners steal behind their torturers' backs, while those same torturers destroy their lives, incognito.

In jail, the cleverest inmates—and I was one of them—quickly learn how to loosen the blindfold in order to see what their prison hell is made of. Only during interrogations. The rest of the time, we were stuck with the regulation hood over our heads, or the burlap bag stinking of piss, the uniform of the ones who were kept in solitary. Interrogation meant torture. Moral of the story: in Heaven, all the female inmates knew that the blindfold, which meant no hood or burlap bag, was synonymous with rape. As sordid a relation of cause and effect as they come: the inmate, if she was as agile as she was bold, could make the most of the unique view onto the world the blindfold offered her if she loosened it just a few millimeters. During the eighteen months of my imprisonment I was forced to undergo long sessions of brutal interrogation. My view of the world amounted to a few centimeters of space above the ground, and a few pairs of feet, sometimes with shoes, sometimes without. You have to have survived a place like Heaven to understand how and why a world reduced to an insignificant patch of floor can suddenly become so vital. You have to have a real hunger for life, in spite of Heaven, to be able to capture that random shot of a pair of feet that spend more time kicking you than walking by. The net of your blurred gaze beneath the blindfold is the only thing connecting you to the world, and most of the time it is reduced to a pair of boots, shoes, or worn-out old slippers splattered with blood, snot, or puke. To survive in Heaven you learn to read the infinitesimal, in spite of yourself. A few foot movements which you then classify according to walk. Even if it's only a few steps forward or back. Traces on the ground . . . Insignificant clues to start with but which over time turn out to be far more eloquent than you would have thought. Rhetoric that is inconceivable outside of isolation. Because freedom doesn't necessarily make you observant. Any more than confinement will ineluctably turn you into a moron. In the deafening world of a prison, where human beings with the power of speech no longer speak, but vociferate, bellow, and scream—some from pain, others to inflict terror and pain—any intelligible element becomes a tool for survival. In Heaven, deciphering the cement floor is the most tenacious road to escape. Thinking allows you to resist, to contain your fear. And on rare occasions to force it over to the other side. So the codebreakers of the interrogation room floor—and I was one of them—had a head start on the others. If you could read the ground, you could be informed. It was a tiny wedge against absolute isolation. You quickly learned that a floor splattered with blood or smeared with shit, urine, or cum was just as eloquent as one wiped with bleach. You could go on to decipher the veiled messages these traces left behind. A pool of blood or urine, drops of blood or cum, a streak of blood or vomit spoke volumes about the torturers' mood, as well as the ordeal your comrades had been through. After the rapes they would mop the floor with the bleach of ritual ablution, and haloes of white foam remained, furrows of macabre still lifes, signs the inmate was scared shitless. Scared shitless before torture, and after. Clues that, like news flashes, regularly punctuated the cadence of the rape and sexual torture, the beatings, the miscarriages. A persistence that narrated the agenda of the days to come. In Heaven, the ground—pure or impure—was a silent screen where a new type of reality show played to an absent audience.

The floor in Heaven, or the dazibao *of psychedelic drawings. No comment. The floor in Heaven needed no words, but it twisted the soul. In Heaven, a man's walk was the ID card of a coward. It was up to the most observant prisoners to identify the jailers and their rank among the despicable. An exploit only the bravest undertook, and for which they paid dearly. We were playing with fire, to be sure, but it was worth it. Even with our shackles, we were better armed against the enemy we had tracked down. Even if he was invisible, and armed with every right including that of beating a prisoner to death, he became vulnerable the moment we could see through to the slightest weakness. There were voices, too, and we could try to make out who they belonged to, these louts who held our lives in their hands. But voices were unreliable. Even the keenest sense of hearing could not unravel the sophisticated effects of the microphones used in Heaven. The only thing I could rely on were the motions that went into a person's walk. Tell me how you walk and I will tell you who you are. I was good, very good at the game. The best. If there was a competition for identifying walks, I would win it every time.*

Only sticklers for detail, and the most determined, dared to defy the anonymity of Heaven's torturers. To differentiate if not distinguish a faceless ghost whose body is reduced to a pair of feet—for that is all that is visible, under certain angles and at rare moments—requires unflagging patience. Heroic, flawless vigilance. I spent hours on the trail of those insignificant little details which could identify a person's walk. The way they took their momentum, then the position of the foot, before, during, and after each kick delivered to my side, or another woman's. The symmetry or asymmetry of the feet—spread, together, parallel—when the guy began to piss on me or my neighbor . . . I can recall the pedal identity of some of them. The dragging slide of the least ferocious guard, whom I eventually managed to win over. He brought me paper and a pencil, and I would write down stories about djinns for him, something he couldn't get enough of. For the best stories I was entitled to a blank sheet of paper. For me alone. They fired him after three months. I swallowed all the sheets with the poems I had written for Del. One day a garden will grow in my belly. With bushes and flowers made of recycled paper, page after page of ragged words of love, words that have been flayed, and I fear they are repugnant, scribbled with tears of blood. I also recall the jerky, careless walk of the three rapists—criminals who were pardoned in return for services rendered—and whom I infuriated with my silence. I could recognize them today by their footsteps alone. I had the time, ample time, to observe the awkwardness of men unused to military boots. Consequently, they were the only ones who walked around barefoot after they'd done their job. To relax. To stretch out their arches, which were numb and needy after all the kicks they'd delivered. Toward the end of my imprisonment, by means of a multitude of painstakingly classified details, I could anticipate their depraved mood, and how they would set about breaking me. Just one glance at the knots in their shoelaces, or the absence of knots, was enough to inform me how the roles had been distributed. Who would beat me, who would rape me or masturbate, with his prick in my face, who would stand back and have a smoke and play the voyeur. I could tell down to the last detail which one would use my body as an ashtray. Whether he would decide to stub out his cigarette on my navel, or whether he would go for the anus.

But the passage of the man who had come into the interrogation room a few hours before my transfer was too brief. His feet only crossed the demarcation line of my visual field for an instant. I noticed, or thought I noticed, the particularity of his walk because his right foot was slightly twisted. This image, the last one granted to me to see in Heaven, remains blurry. A rather vague memory of the feet of a lame duck. But a persistent memory. Shaped, perhaps, by imagination. It's not impossible.

Sitting astride, hands bound by handcuffs behind my back, the blood pouring from me. From everywhere. From every hole in my benumbed body. My nose. My ears. My mouth. My vagina.

There were three of them laying into me. Beating me. Taking turns. I was waiting for whatever was next. One of them might masturbate between my breasts, the other would piss on me, or the other way around. The door creaked open. Someone snapped his fingers. I had blood in my eyes but I could see his boots. Perfectly polished. The laces tied American-style. I saw that he was holding his feet the way an actual soldier would. He snapped his fingers again. My torturers in their grubby slippers disappeared from the few square centimeters that were visible from under the blindfold. The boots of the finger-snapping man reappeared. Planted there before me. I picked myself up, to prepare for the next round of blows. Nothing. No brutality. Just steps creaking behind my back. All four of them were behind me. Moving around. One of them grabbed my hands. The other removed my handcuffs. The sound of metal thrown on the floor was stifled by a roar. The head rapist. The one who opened the door, announced the news, got the ball rolling. You're going to be transferred, you filthy whore. Good riddance. You were starting to piss us off. You don't talk. You refuse to confess. Too bad for you. I felt like shouting in his face, To hell with you! That would be too great an honor. I said nothing. I thought, Better to die than to betray. What did you expect, you little rat? That I would hand my love over to you? I'd rather disappear. They put the hood over me. Then the burlap bag on top of that, stinking of blood, piss, cum. Out you go. They shoved me outside. I could hardly stand. The man with the boots stopped me from falling, helped me out. I thought, The silent woman of Heaven is going to die. They don't need her anymore. They've already killed her love. Del has been executed, that's all. That's why there's all this commotion. From the hell that is Heaven you can only be transferred to the devil. That's what this is all about.

I collapsed. I would have so liked to believe in the hereafter. That way my death would restore me to my love . . . Were they taking me directly to the slaughterhouse? A summary execution in the middle of the night? Like thousands of others sent to the devil by the snapping fingers of the Supreme Commander. No one would be any the wiser. That was what I hoped with all my strength. I wanted to get it over with. Someone, down here, or up there, or with the devil, had heard me. They were going to shoot me in the mouth. That was how they executed those who refused to confess to their crimes. Yes, I was going to die. I felt calm. At peace. The thought of my mother scarcely affected me. She would receive a certificate, stamped by a coroner in the pay of the regime. My death would be certified authentic. And I would sleep. At last. For a long time. With or without Del. It hardly mattered now. The lack of sleep had driven me crazy. I wanted to rest. I wanted to know the serenity of oblivion. Silence, I would sleep for all eternity. Peace in my body and in my mind. No more rape. No more cigarettes on my nipples. No more urine and sperm in my face.

I was curled up in a ball on the backseat of a Patrol. I recognized the sound of the engine. We were going incredibly fast. Destination: deliverance. Was it the finger-snapping man who was driving? Had he been assigned to finish me off? Or had he entrusted me to one of his underlings? I couldn't hear him. It was as if he wasn't breathing. As discreet as a Sioux, driving like a madman. Fine by me. Let him hurry. Fast. Faster. I can't remember anything else. I must have passed out.

Tell me how you walk and I will tell you who you are. The Colonel has returned from the toilets. I am trying to concentrate. I'm staring at the ground, following his steps. His left foot, not his right, slightly turned out . . . No, it's the right foot. I'm getting muddled. It's hard to tell. I can't concentrate. I'm out of practice. My eyes have gone lazy. He sits back down. The boss tells him we have nearly finished. The Colonel doesn't react. He's resigned. And I feel calm again. I must have been hallucinating. Yes, that's it. I should never have agreed to fill in for someone else.

It's been a rotten day, my Vima. Quite a blow. I wish I could swap my life for a few hours with you. I don't like the way things are going. That cop from before was as quiet as a mouse, and I have a bad feeling about him. Not a word at the end of the interrogation. Other than the usual bullshit: We'll keep you informed. When? Will it take long? Can you give me a rough idea? Nothing. The man knows nothing, and won't decide a thing. A rotten day, my Vima. And then, what am I to think of this incredible coincidence? What to make of it? Why have I found myself face-to-face with 455 from Heaven? Isn't it a sign? Of course it is. But it's not a good sign. I'm not particularly paranoid. No one could suspect me of any connection with this woman. No one. Her, of all people. But I believe in signs. Unlike you. If these human rights gentlemen found out that their translator owes her life to us, I could view this coincidence, which is not a coincidence, as a good omen. A good point for me. But can you see me saying to them, Hey, you, do you know where your colleague is from? Do you know how she landed in this country? And even if they do know. Even if they did listen to me, they would never believe that I was her savior. As for her, it would be astonishing if she could envisage such a thing. I'm depressed, Vima. I'm afraid I'll never see you again. I wish I could turn back the clock. I even envy the murderer I used to be. The happiest of men, when he took you in his arms. I have a fever. The way I always do when I relive the inseparable events of my redemption and my misfortune. Five years already, as if it were yesterday. Five years I've been in a coma. Sick with missing you.

I was asleep. A sudden weight pressing on my chest. Metal. Cold as death. A weapon? I woke up with a start. You were leaning over me. Furious. Your face distorted. A grimace of rage. With your palm you slapped the laptop you'd pressed on my chest. I immediately understood. You'd seen the film of 455's interrogation. How could I have forgotten to switch off the computer? Was it subconsciously intentional? Surely. I must have been fed up with the lies. I was petrified and relieved at the same time. Now you knew everything. You had unmasked me. I begged you to let me explain how . . . You shouted, Shut up. You disgust me. The film doesn't need any explanation. Let's watch it together, this live porn show of yours. And you can tell me whether you raped this poor girl before your worthy colleagues, or after. You must be their boss. You've always been the boss. Isn't that right? My hero, with his medals at the age of seventeen, has a new job: boss for a gang of rapists. Of violent murderers. There's no stopping progress. Meteoric rise! You should have died at the front. I would have been proud to be the widow of an authentic hero, rather than the mother of two children conceived with a murderer! You're lucky they're not at home. But I'm going to call them. We should watch your exploits together, the whole family. Maybe they'd be proud of you after all. Everyone in this fucking country is so proud of the father's heritage! Isn't that right? I'm going to ask my father to go with the children. What do you think? Go on, tell me how you went about it with that poor woman . . .

455 was the prisoner's number, in Heaven. For such a wreck, she was imposing. A heroine, her comrades praised her to the skies. The symbol of the maximum-security section. The Iron Woman of Section 209. A legend who drove the Sardive brothers round the bend. They were criminals who'd been sentenced to death for serial killings. And who were pardoned no sooner

than they'd been arrested. Transferred to Heaven from Alabi, the prison for common-law detainees. They were retrained as model torturers. Put in charge of Section 209. Where the hard cases and the silent ones are kept. The ones who take their time before cracking. A luxury they pay for, dearly. They all end up confessing to everything and its contrary. Denouncing friends and strangers. The Sardive brothers' shock treatment can't be beaten. They never fail, with anyone. Even the most stubborn, they can break them down. Make them sign confessions the authorities have typed up ahead of time. 455 was the only one who stood up to them. They let her have it. To no avail. Her silence was driving them up the wall. This girl's silence was the kind that could make you crazy, even some of the other female inmates. She spoke to no one. No one heard her shout. In spite of the torture. She must have been screaming her suffering inside. She was a mystery to everyone, this woman with her gaping wounds. They called her the Crimson Woman—mute, a tombstone, a bleeding ghost. The only one who didn't moan. Because she had nothing of the compliant victim about her. She wasn't the kind that ordinary decent people might eventually help. The silence of 455 deprived the torturers of their right to exist. Her silent scorn was of the kind that merely enraged those who were already overexcited, and made them shout louder than ever. And also made them lose their hard-on. This skinny little woman, standing up to them. While others begged, and hoped if not for clemency at least for an ounce of pity, she opposed her absolute silence. No one had ever seen anything like it. The only word anyone had ever heard from her was *no*. Addressed to no one in particular. A *no* that was ejected from deep in her guts. That escaped from telluric depths. From the bowels of mother earth. 455's *no* was not an answer but a call. Wolves baying at the full moon. A warrior's thunder. An invitation to an ancestral combat. This fury's *no* caused Heaven to tremble from the very first night of her imprisonment. In the middle of the night. A *no* like a brass band, intermittent, high-pitched, shattering the darkness. A voice that carried. The first *no*, delivered in that stentorian voice, grave and clear, shook Heaven until they had to lock the woman up, her feet and wrists bound, an adhesive bandage over her mouth. Since then, the salvos of 455 have haunted the entire establishment. It is as if the walls of Heaven—the solitary cells, the torture chambers, the corridors and latrines—have been impregnated with that *no*. As if Heaven were no more than a sound box for the echo of this extraordinary woman's absolute refusal. A *no* against the intolerable. That was what her co-detainees affirmed. Some of the jailers said Heaven would never erase it from their memory. Just as I could never erase your screams of indignation. Like 455, your anger is proof against time.

Your cries were piercing my eardrums. You wouldn't let up. You condemned me. Again you said, So it's your business to rape women in your filthy prisons, is that it? You left the Army to become a pimp for the torturers of Heaven? That's how you've earned us this palace. You were shrieking. Relentlessly. We had no close neighbors, their requisitioned villas were fairly isolated. I was all the more afraid that I too might be watched over by another of the Commander's henchmen. Which would have made perfect sense, and the thought made my blood run cold. I was fit for hanging and you . . . you, the wife of the worst sort of traitor, you would be handed over to the Sardive brothers. Just the thought that anyone might touch you or hurt you drove me crazy. I slapped you, several times. I shouted, Since when have you been spying on me? Have you forgotten who I am? I am the Commander's soldier! I was waving my arms, my hands pointing to the lampshades, the chandelier, the floor, my terrified gaze was begging you to be quiet. I was trying to make you understand that the house might be bugged. My efforts were futile. You went on screaming and struggling. I tied your hands with my belt. Bound you to the headboard of the bed.

Rammed a fold of the sheet into your mouth. Terror was spilling from your lovely golden eyes. Was I going to kill you? Rape you before killing you? No one has ever known how to speak to me with their gaze the way you could. I didn't have time to reassure you, my love. I sprang to my feet. Left you to your terror and got busy. I went over the villa and the garden with a fine-tooth comb. Computers, laptops, telephones, televisions, household appliances . . . It can be useful sometimes to be really good at your job. I left nothing up to chance. Once I had taken the automatic sprinkler device apart, I collapsed under the arbor and cried like a baby. Uncontrollably. I could rest easy. There were no informers in our house. That took the cake! That pervert Commander's trust in me was absolute. I couldn't stop laughing. He was more unhinged than I thought. This was the clue that pointed to his end. The fact that he could trust me, when you didn't trust me anymore! I was losing my nerves. I started crying again. But these tears were tears of joy. The joy of knowing you were not in danger. I calmed down before I went to join you. You were very upset. Waving your arms like a maniac. You were having trouble breathing. When you saw me you were petrified. Like some sacrificial lamb. But you immediately got hold of yourself. The rage in your eyes as you stared at me, unblinking. Even though your mouth was taped shut I could hear you roaring, Go on, rape me before you bleed me. I looked away and began shouting in turn, like a wounded animal. How could you imagine such a thing. Did you really think I would ever hurt you? Have I ever taken you without your consent? You know very well I need the glue of your desire, a reflection of my own, to make love to you. Your gaze grew harder. The shards of your scorn wounded me. All I inspired in you was disgust and terror. I sprang to my feet. Hurried down the stairs. Rushed into my study. Grabbed my pistol. Standing opposite you with my gun pointed at my heart, I told you that I would not let you go until you had listened to me. If you refused,

I would press the trigger. All I wanted was for you to listen to me. Then you could do as you like. You narrowed your eyes. The sign of a cease-fire. I began talking. Nonstop. A torrent of words. Unleashed, they went wild. I pressed the gun against my heart whenever they hurt me. When they betrayed me, or jeered at me, or escaped from me. How could I find the right words to explain what that invisible snare was like, how I was caught, suffocating, in the mesh of the Lord's army, under the orders of the Supreme Commander? What good would it do, to chatter away about the ins and outs of the profession to which I had been chained for life? You have to have lived inside the whole padlocked system, to find yourself cornered by it. It leaves you no choice. I spoke slowly. Got it all out. One sentence after the other, weighing every word, every detail which might be fatal for you if I were found out. Anything you must not know I kept silent. You already knew too much. You had seen a film you should never have seen. You were already in danger. And I was prepared to die to ensure your safety. I swore to you that I had never killed anyone, never tortured even the tiniest insect, never touched another woman since we got married. How could I, I was crazy about you. You knew that. Once my long entreaty was over, I fell silent. A septic tank, drained. Yes, that's exactly how it felt. I'd been relieved of the weight of my bad conscience. I was docile now, prepared to accept whatever fate you had in store for me. You nodded your head. I untied you. Freed your mouth. You coughed. Took a deep breath. Disappeared into the bathroom. I could hear the water running. I could smell your perfume, intoxicating. I could imagine your gestures. I saw them. You were splashing yourself with water, then rosewater, alternately. Abundantly. To dispel the stench of Heaven that clung to your skin. I wished I could do likewise. To no avail. The pestilence was inside me. An integral part of my being. Injected into the pores of my skin. You came back out. Your hair was wet, disheveled. I could die of desire for you. But I knew I was doomed. Love was forbidden to me. In a neutral voice you asked me to leave you alone. You would come and get me.

I took refuge in the garden. It had been snowing all week long. A thick layer of powdery snow covered the trees, the lawn, the swimming pool. A pale shroud. The branches of the fir trees bent to the weight of the ice crystals. I buried my head in the pine branches. Rubbed my face. I stripped off my clothes and with my bare hands I attacked the sheet of ice which covered the swimming pool. I pounded it with my fists. With the flat of my hands. With my elbows. I pounded until I could scarcely breathe. The surface began to crack, then gave way, streaked with the blood flowing down my fingers. I pretended to ignore my reddened hands. They made me think of the Sardive brothers' hands. I had to wash. To purify myself. To disappear. To see your gaze no longer. Your eyes black with disdain. Your scornful grimaces. I had to get away from your voice calling me a murderer. I plunged into the icy water. It took my breath away. I was gasping for air. I was chilled to the bone. Sinking. And yet the weather was fine. The sun was at its zenith. There were colorful figures all around the swimming pool. I recognized the doctor, his wife and son. They were laughing hysterically. I called out to them: Help, I'm drowning. They didn't see me. Or maybe they were pretending, ignoring the intruder that I was. The despoiler. The doctor's wife, a tall, elegant, beautiful woman, her arms bare in her chiffon dress, was pointing at something. The servant came out with a tray of refreshments. The doctor put his arm around a little brunette with mischievous eyes. He introduced her as his future daughter-in-law. The guests came closer, surrounding them. Moths drawn to a candle flame. I went deeper, paralyzed. I could hear joyful cries, congratulating the fiancés. That's what it was, an engagement party. For the eldest son. Now I remembered. It was the last party held in the garden. I was witnessing the last moments of happiness for the famous surgeon's family. Two days after the party the fiancé was arrested.

Parents, friends, and neighbors were completely taken aback. Why? The boy had never been in trouble. He was handsome. Gentle. An angel. A young man who despised violence. He didn't get involved in politics. No one knew of any suspicious activities. He had no police record, anywhere. Not a single file that might look bad. The brilliant boy was studying architecture, he was a citizen above all suspicion. Why? Why had he been arrested? This was Year One of the Theological Republic, established in the name of God. Peaceful gatherings were forbidden, in the name of God. Protesters were immediately viewed as traitors, Judases in the pay of the aggressor. The witch hunt against counterrevolutionaries had begun, upon the orders of the Commander and by the will of God. The country would be purged of refractory elements of every stripe, thanks to the help of God. Any individual manifesting suspicious behavior in a time of war was punishable by execution upon the very place of arrest, without any other form of trial, and with the consent of God. Since the ultimate judge could only be God. Amen. The staff announced the Commander's edict at the front. I admired the wisdom of our leader, the head of our armies. As did all the volunteers in the militia. We were prepared, as one man, to take any high-ranking army officer educated under the former regime who did not share our point of view and kill him on the spot. This law, promulgated in record time like all the others, was necessary to save the Fatherland.

We were just poor, foolish adolescents, easy to manipulate. We were just poor, ignorant peasants whom an old man with a hard heart had turned into fools, without even having to give it much thought. We made good cannon fodder. The doctor's son, like thousands of others, was ripe for hanging. The clerics in charge had set up the altar where they would sacrifice the country's youth. In the name of God and by the will of the Commander. After six months of desperate searching, the doctor found out his son had been killed. Shot in someone else's place. I knew all this when I agreed to move into the villa. You are right, Vima, I'm a murderer, I'm no better than they are. You are right, Vima, it's not enough not to have used your own hands to kill, that does not absolve you. You are right, Vima, I am their accomplice . . .

I can hear the echo of your screaming again. You went crazy. Get out. Get out of there, right now. You threw the garden hose at me. I still don't know how with your weak arms you pulled me out. I woke up around noon. In a sweat. A cold sweat. With a terrible headache. You left me some medicine, a thermos of tea, and a note on the night table: "You have to leave. Get the hell out. You have to leave those monsters and this country. Otherwise, I'm the one who will leave you. I'll come back tomorrow morning so we can talk about it."

Now here I am all alone in the world in a sordid room in a center for homeless refugees. For five years I've been trying to hang on. In vain. I don't lie anymore. I don't get my hands dirty. I denounce our tyrants. For five years I've been telling them I'm ready to speak openly to the cameras. In public. To journalists from all around the world. If they extend their human rights to me, and valid documents. The truth doesn't pay. No more here than it does there, my Vima. Yuri is one of those guys with a library for a brain, and he has sworn to me that the democrats here are all hand in glove with the tyrants there and everywhere else. They have breakfast with Putin. They have lunch with emissaries from the Supreme Commander. Dinner with Kim Jong-il. They smoke their cigars with Castro and fuck the young whores—blondes, brunettes, blacks—they are offered wherever they go. Could be. Yuri knows what he's talking about.

It's been a rotten day, my Vima. I'll go and see him to get my mind on other things. If he's in a bad mood, we'll brood together. Yuri does nothing but read. He's been vegetating here for over a year. He tells me I'm the only one who can get him away from his books. It's because I enjoy listening to him. And he likes to talk as much as he likes to read. He's a born storyteller. He has a ton of stories in his head. When he's fed up with me, he starts drinking. In the beginning, I would watch while he polished off one bottle after another, going deeper and deeper. But we haven't gotten drunk together in ages. That's what we'll do tonight. Get wasted and talk about Achilles the invincible. That's one of his best stories. Achilles' heel, according to Yuri, is the symbol of a person's fragility in the world. To think I have spent most of my life without ever drinking a drop of alcohol. What a jerk. I would never have made it in this fucking icicle of a country without Yuri's vodka. He tells me, Better late than never, dumbass; bottoms up.

I leave the office. In a hurry. With only one thing on my mind, to climb into bed with a book. To forget this entire day. And yet my legs, these bloody legs that don't always obey me, are leading me elsewhere. Dragging me into the center of town where the shrink's office is. That's where I am now. In a sweat. Out of breath. I'm going up the stairs four at a time. I don't have an appointment. Never mind. Here I am. I have my reasons. It's obvious. I've just confronted my past. The shrink will be proud of me. I have to tell him the good news. It's only normal. He'll approve. I ring the bell. The secretary says, but you don't have an appointment! I know. It's urgent. I'll wait. Until the last hour if need be. It's important. It's absolutely vital. I must look weird. She doesn't answer. She stares at me. Doesn't smile. I leave her where she is standing in the entrance hall. I go and collapse on the sofa next to the door to the consulting room. That way he can't miss me. He always sees his patients to the door. The last one leaves at 7:45 P.M. Two hours and then some, and the whole time I sit mentally revising everything I have to tell him. Here he is at last. I stand up. He doesn't have much time for me. I bark that it's all right, and I thank him, and I think that not much time will be more than enough to tell him about this incredible encounter. Five minutes will be enough. Now I'm lying down. Five minutes go by before I can say a single word. Then I speak and hear myself all at the same time. I can hear my voice getting ahead of my thoughts. My voice spilling out secrets I didn't mean to reveal. There's nothing for it.

On it goes. Not a word about my day. Or the Office. Or the Colonel. The past I have just confronted rises up before me. But the way it wants to. There is no one else in the background, only him. Del. My love. My wound. My failure to understand. Del who disappeared. The silence that kills. My refusal to live. Overwhelmed by grief, by absence. Where are you, my beloved?

The voice in me talks to the shrink as if to a friend. Calls him by his first name, to my great surprise. I never told you how I got out of the country. I have very confused memories of the final moments of my imprisonment. And there are black holes regarding what came next. It all happened so very quickly. I can't remember a thing about how I left the country. How I ended up here, in your country. A place I knew nothing about. I'm a child of the sun, the desert, and now here I am in this glacis of fjords. Snatches of events without any apparent link coalesce in my mind then disappear. I clutch at a series of images. And the sensory markers which connect them. More precisely, there are two negatives, as if from a film. As if they were imprinted on my flesh. The first is that of my body covered in blood and curled up in a corner of my cell. And in the second, I have been propelled onto the back seat of a Patrol. The link between the two is the invisible man who sprang me from prison with a snap of his fingers. As simple as that. Just a few snaps of the fingers. I am trying to reconstruct it all, as if with computer-generated images. My eyes are like the computer screen where I have sketched the identikit of my savior thanks to my corporeal memory. Hearing replaces eyesight. I imagine him to be tall and thin, even bony, with square hands and protruding eyes. Features inspired by the abrupt, rhythmic clicking of his fingers. Features that would suit an unremarkable sort of man. Which doesn't necessarily justify the protruding eyes. And then I see myself, a dark tangled mass wedged in a fetal position onto the backseat of the powerful car. When the joyride began, I disconnected, I was tossed about, filled with vague sensations, my psyche cut in two. Fear in my belly and a desire to die. Animal instinct and human thought are rarely compatible when one is aware of impending death. Except when a vital need for rest overpowers everything else. Eradicates fear. Lulled by the purr of the engine and the thought of this salutary death, I passed out. I came to in a bed. A clean bed. Sheets that smelled of my grandmother. I wasn't at home. Or at my mother's place. But in a hospital, or a clinic. The light was gentle, dim. A greenish light. It hardly lit up the room. I had needles in my veins, and tubes hooked up to transfusion devices next to the bed. I had trouble keeping my eyes open. There were shadows and silhouettes, smiles and moving lips. They faded, then were interspersed with each opening of my eyelids. Hands busy with me. Examining me. Blood pressure. Pulse. Injection. Then they tucked me in. Gone the torturers and the rapists. Farewell, solitary confinement. White coats, taking care of me. But not speaking to me. Whispering among themselves, smiling, writing who knows what onto papers removed from one file and put back in another. Where am I? Who are you? No answer. Just lips palpitating in the doorway. I had difficulty reading them. Were they addressing me or someone else? A multitude of hidden, invisible people? Yes, I could hear a voice repeating the same sentence at regular intervals. You are here to rest. You are extremely weak. Like a sound track. A recording. As if they were making fun of me. As if it were all an act. Were there any other patients in this hospital? Any other broken bodies? People wrenched from that dump, Heaven, like me? Did the white coats know where I'd come from? Were they the healers of the tortured women of Heaven, escaped from hell? Or were they angels? Was I dead? No. I knew I wasn't. But I didn't know whether I was right in my head. I asked them. Once again their closed mouths were suggestions and smiles. When I pressed them, one of them gave me an injection. Another one stroked my cheek with all the tenderness in the world. I could hear a man's voice. He said, Put plasters on the soles of her feet. He must have been the doctor. My feet were in shreds, torn to bits, I knew that. The Sardive brothers were experts at flagellation, and they used only electric cables to whip us. They had a preference for the palms of the hands and the soles of the feet, starting with the fingertips. The doctor said, Change her bandages every hour, and leave her feet to air for ten minutes. Someone whispered, she has such little feet. That's what he used to say. Del would say, You have the prettiest little feet in the world. Another injection. More caresses. And I dozed off, and on my feet I was wearing the red sandals he had given me on one of our sun-filled trips. I fell asleep. I slept with my little feet bound in red sandals. Lulled by the scattered words of my love, "an apple . . . an orange . . . I cannot . . . your feet . . . stamping the floor . . . " It was gentle. So gentle when he spoke to me. It was perfect. Out of paradise.

I awoke—after I don't know how many hours or days—and my mother was by my side. How could this be? Prisoner number 455 from Section 209 of Heaven Prison was entitled to a visit from her mother! Was I at the prison infirmary? Was I about to go back to the men who raped me, their spit, their inflamed members? No. I was not in the kennel for battered dogs which they wrongly called an infirmary. But in a clinic worthy of the name. Who had informed my mother? Who had told her where I was? Who had allowed her to come and visit me? What had I done to earn the right to such privileges? It was the sort of favor that stank of collaboration. Had I sold our friends for the sake of my grandmother's clean sheets? My mother swore to me that I hadn't, and she never lies. Her ravaged face came close to mine. Her breath, stinging me. I heard her praying. She spoke to me of a miracle. A providential man. A savior. She blessed him. Her prayers would go with him all her life. I was stunned. Exhausted. Drugged. I left my other questions for later. Shortly afterwards, I found myself in another bed. Another room with a high, gleaming ceiling. No more white coats. No more needles in my veins. No more drips. My mother was still there with me. She was washing me while she spoke. She said, We'll leave as soon as you're on your feet. In a week or ten days at the most. We're going to leave the country. You will be free at last, and safe. I gathered all my strength. All my strength to say no. *A clear, short, irreversible* no. *That famous* no, *the envy of all my companions in misfortune. Those two letters which elevated me to the status of the heroine of Heaven. No, I won't go anywhere without him. I will never leave the country, never abandon him to the vultures. My mother said, He'll get out. The man promised. Del will join you. I swear. He told me he would.*

For a long time my mother's tears had no longer been salt but bitter. Like bitter almonds. No, concentrated opium. An acrid, viscous taste, which stung my palate. I'll never get rid of the taste. I know that. I already told you, Doctor. From the first bite my food takes on the taste of her tears. Moldy, with an aftertaste of bile, just so I don't forget. Never forget anything. How much longer did I go on sleeping in that spacious room with its large picture window, overlooking a garden? All that remains of the den of my last, clandestine days in my forbidden country are the pearly ceiling and my mother's tears, overflowing, submerging me. I see her again, waving a piece of paper in front of my face and saying, You didn't want to trust your poor mother. Look. Open your eyes, wide. You recognize Del's handwriting, don't you? Read it. Read what he says. I looked away. My mother's frozen expression and her conniving smile exasperated me. It was a theatrical mask, lifeless. Writing is falsification. Starting with the holy scriptures. The dictatorship of God teaches us this, at our expense. No. I do not trust writing or signatures. Any more than I trust voices. I have held in my hands dozens of pages of confessions supposedly signed by friends or by Del. Certified by God! I did not trust them at all. In those latitudes, everything is faked. Everything is lies . . . They would say, You can see it's your terrorist husband's handwriting. You see, he has confessed to his crimes. Don't tell me you're blind, you scumbag. Not yet anyway. You can see his signature at the bottom of the page. Go on pretending you're blind and I will personally gouge out your eyes, you whore. Sign at the bottom of the page and you will be free. To my mother I said, I don't want your paper. I don't trust signatures. She begged me, Read the message and then decide. It's the man who saved you who brought it to me. My tears flowed in spite of myself. Del, my love, my man, my husband in chains. I trembled. I grabbed the paper from her hands. Skimmed it, just to put my mind at rest: "Get out as soon as you can. Go away. Leave the country. I will join you. Djadjal." My eyes opened wide. Djadjal was a password that only he and I knew. Had there not been this secret code, the stamp of love, I would have gone on saying no *until I was blue in the face. I would have shouted it so loudly that he would have heard. But this note really was from Del. He was the one who was ordering me to leave, who was promising to come and find me. I looked at my mother and said, All right, we'll leave. She burst into tears. Did not even try to hide them. They were tears of joy but tears all the same. Get some rest now, she said. You have to be in shape for the departure. Where? How? Who with? Don't worry about a thing. He will bring us some fake ID papers that will open the way to freedom. He? She didn't know anything more than that. It was better not to know. To respect the golden rule of safety through anonymity. Until further notice. When Del came to find me, he would explain the miracle.*

Between my leaving the clinic, the days I spent in my savior's hiding place, and my presence in this new country where the days seem long, seem endless, there are only black holes. Absences. Forgetting. And abscesses of violence. My mother went home after several months had gone by. She would have liked to stay a bit longer to take care of me. But they wouldn't renew her tourist visa. As for me, I put on the garments of the stateless refugee, for I had no other choice. Exile is a dizzying ordeal. And if you are far from your beloved, it is bound to be agony. Since I arrived here I have been shoring up my life, Doctor. Del's absence grew longer. Week after week. Month after month. A year went by. My mother kept me waiting as best she could. With her weekly phone calls. Her empty promises. Apparently there were complications. His escape would be soon. He was going to come. Be patient, she said. Don't lose hope . . . A year and five months. I couldn't stand it anymore. I called her in the middle of the night. I'm coming home, Mama. I don't want this freedom if he's not part of it. Unless he's dead. Tell me, I beg you, if they have executed him. He's dead and you don't dare tell me? Disorientated, up against the wall, at last she confessed the truth. Del is alive. But he won't be coming, my dear. He won't come. He was released a while ago. No one knows exactly when. Neither his parents nor your savior. The man just told me that after his release he disappeared. He's in the country. But no one knows where he lives. My mother had lied to me out of love. To protect me. The way I've been lying to you for three years, Doctor. I was lying to you when I said they executed him. I too was lying to you, out of love for him. I was hoping to protect him, to keep him intact. The way it was, when we were happy. I stopped tormenting my poor old mother with my questions. She still doesn't know where he is. I took the time I needed to find out what I could, even if I still don't know exactly where he is living. I contacted former comrades through secret channels. Took every precaution. And I learned what I would rather never have known, my whole life long. My husband was no longer in chains even when I still was. He was released before the providential man saved me. My Del. My tall, strong man. My idol. My life. My reason for living. He knew all about my ordeal. He could not help but know what I was going through. And yet he deserted me. Abandoned me. When he knew everything. He condemned me to exile. A double exile, and he was the cause of it. Why, Doctor? Why? I'm trying to understand. I have to understand. Or maybe I'm actually refusing to understand. I'm afraid of the truth. This tenuous link between Del and the finger-snapping man terrifies me. Was Del a stool pigeon, in the service of my mother's providential man? If so, did he betray others to save me? . . . Impossible. Since he was released before I was. I cannot . . . I cannot believe they made him into their flunky. I was crushed. I wept, Doctor. I wept. I thought there were no more tears in me. I will never get over this. I have been mortified for life. I'm so afraid. You can see for yourself, I'm still crying. I'm calling him Doctor now, no more first names. The shrink says, We'll stop there. What you have just told me is of prime importance. And moreover, you master the language perfectly. I will see you tomorrow. We have to go deep into the heart of your trauma.

Now I am outside and I'm still crying. I'm walking. Weaving my way through the crowd, with my head down. I cry. All the way home. Nine kilometers of tears. Without his pebbles Tom Thumb is lost, adrift. On the razor's edge, the path of exile. The snowy path of this elsewhere at the end of the world, looking out onto nothingness.

In the icy bathroom, with all the rage of despair I rub my aching limbs and think of what my shrink has said. I didn't waffle at all today. That truly was a first. I didn't have to go hunting for my words. I speak the language of exile perfectly. But I haven't incorporated it. I don't feel at home in it. I don't like the harsh sounds of this strange, indefinable language. I have no affinity, no intimacy with the coarse speech and irascible expressions of these polar islanders. I'm not at ease. And yet today I surpassed myself. Without realizing it. Does language, any language, flow more easily when the subject is love?

For how many years have I been coming to these sessions? So, for three years I have been cheating. Keeping silent about an emotional trauma. That's what the shrink said. Yes, something like that. I refused to talk about the pain I was carrying. I emphasized the rapes, the imprisonment, my homesickness in order to cover up the abandonment. Del abandoned me. My love abandoned me. The crux of the hurt. All the rest is paraphrase. I rub between my legs until I bleed. I tell myself that the worst of it is that I will never know why or how I was spared, protected, saved.

I'm going to go and talk to her. Yes, I will go and find the translator in the park. She goes there every Sunday. To the Leibzen Park. I've been following her for weeks. I know her habits. How she spends her free time. Her handful of friends. I say friends, but they may only be colleagues. Vague acquaintances. The former bait 455 goes running every day. She often goes to the cinema. Alone. She spends hours in museums. Occasionally with someone. She spends her Sundays in the park. She goes jogging. Walks for half an hour. Stretches out on a bench when it's not freezing. Otherwise, she passes her time in one of the cafés around the park. She always has a pile of newspapers and several books, and goes back and forth reading them. With her pencil in her hand. She often marks the pages which claim her attention. I had decided to wait for her outside her neighborhood cinema, but then in the end I opted for the park. Tomorrow, Sunday, I'll go and speak to her. Tell her everything. I have taken notes, so I won't forget anything. Perhaps I'll begin with the end. With our argument, my Vima. Or should I say, my end. With you gone, I'm not living. I'm vegetating. I'll begin with the moment our fates were sealed, entwined. Our quarrel and her salvation. Thanks to you, my Vima, she escaped death. In fact, I'll begin with you. Here's what I'll tell her: You owe your life to my wife.

I remember every moment of that night and the rush of days before I fled. You saved me from drowning and you went to live with your father, to be with the children. You came back the next day. At around noon. Without the children. I was relieved. I thanked you for saving me . . . You interrupted my futile words. You wanted to go straight to the heart of the matter. You wanted to know all about the prisoner. You said, Above all don't lie. What crime did that girl commit to deserve that? You pointed to the CD you had left on the night table. You went on in a sinister voice, We'll watch it together, since you brought it into our home. I began spouting out information, as if I were in the presence of a superior. A salutary form of conditioning from my job. It was the only way to stay on course. You did not take your eyes off me.

The prisoner has been put on file as a first class bait, and given the number 455. Her true identity is not to be found in any of the prison records. Solely in the central files at Security. Prisoners belonging to this category are always arrested in the same manner. The individual . . . You got exasperated, you interrupted, tersely, This one happens to have a name, as far as I know. I remained silent for a few seconds. Your gaze was piercing. You knew that her name was Vima, like you. You had heard the Sardive brothers call her Vima the whore. I knew what you wanted. You wanted a substitution to take place. You wanted me to confuse the two of you; had I forgotten that you could be every bit as disconcerting and intransigent as Vima, 455? I started over. Vima must have been arrested by civilians, not agents with a warrant. You pointed out, That's called kidnapping, not arrest. I had to reformulate my words. Vima was kidnapped by agents in civilian clothing, wearing balaclavas. That is the method of arrest used for baits. For the last eighteen months she has been held in Heaven. Her husband was sentenced to fifteen years of prison for subversive activities and plotting against the security of the state, and after his detention in Heaven he was transferred to another maximum security prison. He is suspected of being at the head of a small group of activists. Vima will be used as an instrument to break her husband. You let out a cry of horror. Then you said, Go on. I swear on the life of our children that that is all I know about this woman. You were stunned, and said, And what about this? You waved the CD at me. What is your role in all this? What could I say? I no longer know who I am, nor what I am doing, nor what my role is, as you put it. I murmured, The prison authorities gave me this CD two days ago. They cannot understand how Vima manages to resist. No one resists the Sardive brothers. Vima, the heroine whose lips are sealed, is an extraterrestrial to them. No matter how much they shatter her body, she doesn't flinch. No one has been able to subdue her. It's beyond comprehension. I have to find the breach. You stared at me, wide-eyed. The breach? I said, Yes, the breach which might indicate any eventual complicity. Now your eyes were staring out of your head. A wild, demented look, which disgusted me. You started laughing. The insane laugh of a lunatic. You were on the verge of choking. I shook you violently. You screamed. Do you really mean to say that your idiot superiors actually think she's in cahoots with her rapists? Do you too believe in a complicity between those perverts and this poor woman? I remember how your slender body trembled. A delicate shrub caught in a storm. You said, A demonic system which uses violence will eventually self-destruct. In the meantime I want to watch the CD with Vima 455 again, no matter what. You said you wanted to see me in my element. At my observation post. Yes, you barked, we'll watch your CD in the living room, on the big television screen. I was sweating profusely. Cold sweat down the length of my spine. And you were suddenly so calm again, as you repeated, Let's watch your porn film. With the star who has the same name as me. That should excite you! On you went. In a bland tone of voice. As if you were merely chatting. Innocently. About everyday life. Nothing important. You said, You just do your job. Find the breach. What's behind the failure of these rapists who have run out of ideas? And I will examine the gaping hole inside you, your abysmal lack of humanity. At least I won't do it behind your back! Let's get going. Just pretend I'm not here! I threw myself at your feet. Burst into tears. You pushed me away and screamed. Do you want to know what I think of your position as project manager for the security enhancement of the nation's penitentiaries? It's a job for mental retards. It's just a chore where one group of murderers pays top dollar to another murderer, who has the nerve to think he's above them. The fine gentleman who does not use his own hands to kill. I shouted, Enough, enough, you might as well kill me here on the spot. Or why don't I do it for you, and make things easier for you. You want to die? That's too easy! you said. You have to deserve it. And you added, After all, you're just a poor victim. Yet another. The system is churning them out en masse. In a fractured society, it's the tyrant's privilege to divide people, alienating some of them and crushing others. Then you collapsed, with your full weight. You held your head in your trembling hands. You were weeping. Your tears drove a whirlwind through my heart. You began speaking in a low voice. Exhausted but determined. You said, You have only one solution, and that is to leave. Once you've rescued this woman. You are going to arrange her escape. And her husband's. I don't want to know how you go about it. You must have more than enough power for trifles like this. You said, That's the only way out. They are the ones who will save you, in the end. They're your only chance, if you ever want to see me again. I don't want my children to have a murderer for a father. I will come and join you, and bring them with me, if everything goes well. You said, I'm going to live with my father. You immediately pointed your finger at me. A familiar gesture. Tender. The one you used with the children to make them obey right away. A gesture which meant, if you protest, or talk back, Mama won't speak to you for forty-eight hours. For them that was the worst punishment. As it was for me. I remained silent. You said, I'll be back, in a few days.

I was on it right away, as we say in our jargon. The next

morning at dawn I went to the Circle's headquarters, to the Bureau for officials assigned to Supreme Commander's Residence. I stole a pile of letterhead. Stamped every sheet. Knowing full well that I would be signing my death warrant if I were caught. Then I immediately went home. Started planning my strategy by making a few phone calls, a few debts to call in. They could figure out how to justify my absence for the few days' leave I was granting myself. I set to work. Spent a few hours copying out falsified orders. A few more imitating the signature of the Supreme Commander's private secretary. I racked my brains to come up with a letter that would justify the urgent transfer of bait 455 to the Army Hospital. It was a banal procedure but was meant to be used only in exceptional circumstances. They would set the bait back on her feet out of a concern for profitability, and only if it were truly worth it. I took all the necessary precautions to depict 455 as the brains behind a plot.

Once I'd worked out the scenario, I went to see the examining magistrate for in camera lawsuits. A formidable fellow. A fox. Wary. Suspicious. Lying in wait for his own shadow. Without raising an eyebrow he added the necessary codes for a transfer along with his signature on the back of the warrant and handed it back to me. He didn't ask any questions other than the date of my next trip to Asia. He wanted to place an order with me for some silk for the youngest of his three wives. Done deal. Plus a kimono for Your Honor, your wife will appreciate it, I'm sure. I left him and went to Heaven, impressed by my own daring. I would oversee the transfer in person. Which was less usual, suspicious even. But I had all my alibis to deflect suspicion, not to mention the blessing of the judge, who had called the prison warden. The miracle of the kimono! I put on my officer's uniform. This gave me the authority to silence anyone who might start asking questions. At around six o'clock in the evening I snatched the prisoner from the Sardive brothers' clutches, right in the middle of a torture session. She was in a bad way. I took her straight to the hospital. Left her in the care of one of the most gifted doctors in the unit, reserved for baits.

That same evening I contacted her husband's former lawyer. A so-called "reformed" man. One of those countless independent lawyers who ended up in prison, were tortured and then released on bail. They no longer had the right to practice their profession. I arranged to meet him in a restaurant outside town, and told him what I wanted. Initially for him to get in touch with Vima's mother, and give her a visiting permit for the Army Hospital. I would see him again for the next stage. The poor man was terrified. He began stammering, Why me? He was under surveillance and naturally he was afraid this was a trap. He went pale at the thought that he might get caught and have to go back to prison. I threatened him. Told him I would send him there in person if he didn't cooperate. Then I reassured him. I wanted to help Vima. I told him I was giving him a chance, after a fashion, to practice his profession. Risk-free. I guarantee you. The guy couldn't believe his ears. Who was I to be so sure of what I claimed? His tone became aggressive. A burst of courage, of disguised fear . . . I could easily understand what he was going through. I smiled. I'm on your side now, I said. And I repeated my words, thinking about you, my Vima. On your side. Since this morning, I have been a reformed man. A reformed murderer. I've simply changed sides. Which should be enough of an explanation for you. He didn't dare ask whether my repentance smelled of sulfur the way his did. I told him that as soon as Vima was on her feet, I would obtain false passports for her and her mother. They would have to disappear immediately afterwards. She will refuse to leave without her husband, said the lawyer firmly. Don't worry, he'll be going, too. Sooner or later. But time is of the essence. We have to be quick. Two days later I found out that Vima's husband had been released not long after her arrest. As for their comrades, they were all on file in archive XXII. These are secret archives where undivulged summary executions are recorded. These prisoners are not allowed visits, and their families assume they are still alive. The authorities resort to this cloak to veil their wrongdoings, in order to conceal the astronomical number of executions. I didn't have time to go into the matter. To start looking into those secret files might only attract the attention of any shit-stirrers on my trail. There are plenty of them who would like nothing better than to prove their supremacy when it comes to overzealousness. Anything is permitted if it means getting to blow your trumpet in high places. There was no time to put my mind at rest. In spite of the desire nagging at me, I would never know for sure whether Vima's husband sold his comrades or not. No! Vima's talisman, that word *no*, which was meant to protect him from everyone and everything, did not have the desired effect this time. The question would remain unanswered. In the meantime, I had to be cunning. Hide the truth from Vima. What would she become without that love which made her invincible? The passports were ready. The women would be leaving by land. One of my smugglers would go with them to a border post where the customs officials were not too fussy. But as I suspected, Vima refused to leave the country without her husband. Her mother was in a panic. According to the lawyer, who was on the verge of a nervous breakdown, she wanted to see me. She wanted to have a meeting with her daughter's savior before her daughter got arrested again. I suggested a telephone conversation. I obtained a secure cell phone for her through the lawyer. I called her. Her voice frayed the moment she said her daughter's name. Then came a succession of words in dark colors where a pale ray of hope filtered. Hope in the form of my person. I reassured her. I asked her to be ready for an imminent departure. Del would be joining them. And if he couldn't, I would find a way to persuade Vima to leave the country as soon as possible. I knew what I still had to do. I was perfectly aware of the way things stood. The only one who could persuade Vima to leave the country was Del. Vima drew her strength from this absolute love, she obeyed only the logic of her private, most interior feelings. Her loyalty protected her from everything rotten that lay outside her love. A love she wanted to keep intact. In a pure state. Is it not in the notion of loss that we measure the dizzying intensity of love? And in the hope of meeting again, the strength to go on living? I had just lost you. I was going to wrench myself from you, solely in the hope of finding you again someday. Vima and I would be undergoing the ordeal by fire of our mystics. From that moment on, between myself and that unknown woman who bears your name there was tacit, secret, and no doubt unconscious complicity.

I found Del's address quite easily. A godforsaken place in the east of the country. A village at the edge of the desert where he was living like a hermit. His years in jail had crushed him. Rotten teeth. A hollow gaze. A hunched back. His hair had turned white. I knew exactly what they had put the guy through in order to lobotomize him. To transform a man in his prime into a vegetable. It was plain to see. It wasn't even worth making anything up. He didn't care about any of that. Just what did I want. For him to write a note to Vima. When he heard his wife's name he shuddered. He didn't ask any questions, didn't want any explanation. All I had to do was dictate what he had to write. He grabbed the sheet of paper I held out to him and did as I asked: "Leave the country. I beg you. I will join you. I promise. The man who helped you will do the same for me." I put his note in my pocket. Turned on my heels to hurry away. The man's misery was my own. It went straight to my heart. Vima's broken love sent me back to our tragedy. I fled from him as fast as I could. I was sitting in the car when I saw him running toward me, breathlessly. I rolled down the window. He was gasping. Coughing, and spitting blood. In his rasping voice he said, Give me back the paper, I have to add our code. That way she'll be sure the note is from me. He scribbled "Djadjal" at the bottom of the page and handed it back. I started up without delay, but I could see him standing outside his hut. I thought I could hear him weeping. In fact I was the one who was weeping. I also thought I could see a child in the rearview mirror, going up to him, unsteadily. Then I lost sight of the little toddling creature, clinging to his father's leg.

Tomorrow I will go and look for Vima 455. She will find out who I am at last.

The park is swarming with people. After months of frost and storms the weather is milder. Everyone is venturing outside at last. To smell the first buds after the long hibernation, the favorite ritual of the park regulars. I know them all. Or almost. That's normal, I've been spending practically every Sunday with them for the last three years. These nature enthusiasts have given me the bug. I love the trees with their thick foliage in this old imperial park. Disheveled in winter, majestic in summer. I adore the exotic flowers and the bonsai in the greenhouse. And the two cafés with their windows steamed up, winter and summer alike. I stumbled upon this place by chance. My mother was still here. We were wandering aimlessly, the way exile forces you to do. We suddenly found ourselves outside an impressively high wrought iron gate. Somewhat intimidated, we went through it. And there before me was the wonderland of my childhood fairy tales. An enchanted garden. Splendid. And a greenhouse with exotic plants, which dazzled my mother. For her, the luxuriant flora and the bonsai—something she had never seen—could only be a foretaste of Paradise, confirming the omnipotence of God. We ended our day in one of the cafés in the park. As she drank her steaming hot chocolate, she said tenderly, Look, Vima, the windows are silently weeping. Like us. They have a heavy heart, as we do.

Now in that same café I sense that someone is watching me. I immediately spot the man through the plate-glass window. I seize on the reflection of his tense profile amid the smiling faces. The man is trying to hide. He makes awkward gestures. Near a group of children, playing daddy when he obviously isn't one. He's wearing a cap. His face is wrapped in a scarf up to his eyes. He hovers near the café. Then goes away again. Spins around and comes back toward me. I want to get to the bottom of this. I stand up and leave the café with a determined stride. No, I'm not paranoid. He really is following me. There he is again in the middle of a crowd of people. Then behind the trees. Furtive, wary. He's both hiding and spying. Hunted or hunting? I am the prey. His prey, at least. I must get the predator off my trail. My instinct as a former jailbird once again prevails. This other self who has been living with me since Heaven knows from experience how to get away from the world. How to be absent, the better to grasp everything around her. At the slightest sign of danger she automatically lowers her eyes. And now my vision becomes sharper. Here I am back at my observation post: the ground, and those who are treading on it. Those whom I decipher, anonymously, without being noticed. And in the wink of an eye I have identified that lame duck walk, the Colonel's huge feet. They just barely avoid stepping on the red toenails of a little round foot compressed in a yellow sandal. They follow close on the tiny heels of pretty little Valentina, Peter and Helena's daughter. I recognize her thanks to the red pom-poms on her patent leather shoes. What is this guy doing here? Why is he spying on me? I'm trying to guess what he's up to. Questions and answers collide in my brain. And a rising fear. I acted as his translator, to fill in for someone. Or was it part of a trap? The guy is on a mission. His mission is to eliminate me. The idea, as unfounded as it is absurd, unnerves me. I can feel the panic getting under my skin. Settling there. Irrational. Indomitable. I am free. In a crowded park. I'm surrounded by people. Precisely, that's the problem. I'm a free woman with no resources. No battle plan. No weapon. Blocked. Petrified at the thought of an imminent attack. It spells the end of everything. A wave of panic comes over me. I start to run. He's following me. I am breathless by the time I reach the middle of the bridge connecting the east of the town to the west. I have to slow down. Then I stop. I absolutely have to get to the bottom of this. I have to react.

She turns around, suddenly. Out of breath. I am fifteen feet from her. I freeze. I cannot take another step. She recoils. And says, What do you want from me? I know who you are. Above all, don't come any closer or I'll scream. She is flushed with anger. I have to speak. She mustn't make a scene, whatever the cost. There are policemen patrolling the entire length of the bridge. They've increased surveillance around here ever since the scuffle between hooligans and gypsies shook the entire neighborhood. I have to be quick. This is my only chance to avoid any ID checks. So I say, I would just like to speak to you. I know who you are, too. Not just as a translator. I know your name. I just want to speak to you. She steps further back. And then? she asks. She's going to call out for help. I'm sure of it. I've said too much, or not enough. Then I get an idea. In a flash.

I turn to face him. My head hurts. My brain is about to explode. I have trouble thinking. I'm afraid I'll be cast into the black hole of amnesia. React. Otherwise you'll be sucked in and buried. You're a hair's breadth from lapsing into a waking coma where nothing exists anymore. And you'll lose the thread. So I breathe and think, if this guy has followed me, it's because he has a good reason to. I go closer. Look him straight in the eyes. What do you want from me? I say. To speak to you, I hear him say. I know who you are, too. Not just as a translator. I know your name. I just want to speak to you, says the Colonel again. And then? My voice is trembling. Have I been screaming without realizing it? He has his hands in his pockets. I see his right hand moving, quickly . . . He's going to kill me. I have to call the cops . . . There are fingers dancing before my eyes. He is snapping them, without interruption. The man who is snapping his fingers says, You remember, don't you? The shock is terrible. My heart is pounding fit to burst. I'm going to pass out. I cling to the railing of the bridge, my knees buckle. He comes closer and says, Yes, I'm the one who enabled you to escape. I would just like to speak to you. About the woman who saved your life. I owe you some explanations.

I don't have time to speculate about my initial hunch. I had recognized the feet and the walk of my savior during our first encounter at the Office. And I have not been mistaken in my analysis. I got it right, even though I could scarcely believe it. The asylum seeker and the man who, by snapping his fingers, got me out of Heaven, are one and the same. Is this the vengeance of fate? I raise my head. Look at him. He asks me if I feel all right. Yes, I'm okay. He asks me if he can go on. Yes, he can. So he says, Once you've heard me out, I will just have one favor to ask of you. Not for me. For this person. The one who saved you. I stand up straight. Right in front of him. And look straight at him. I stretch my neck to see him better. I can smell his fetid breath. I feel a surge of nausea in my guts. I collapse again. I put my backpack on the ground. I open it, reach for my water bottle, and empty it. One thought obsesses me, haunts me. This man knows Del. He gave his message to my mother. The man who gives orders with a snap of the fingers knows what my mother did not know. What I could not find out. He knows where Del is. I tell him, I'll hear you out. He's surprised. Or perhaps anxious. He glances at his watch. Gazes furtively around us. He nods. Murmurs, Thanks. But not now. Not here. I'll explain. Tomorrow. Ten o'clock. By the landing stage in the port. The last bar, behind the docks. Is that all right with you? I nod. He disappears in a flash.

Provided she doesn't change her mind. Doesn't flake on me. I sense I don't have much time left, my Vima. They're putting too much pressure on me. But I won't yield. I promised you I would no longer let myself be manipulated, that I would never go back to being a murderer. Ever again. I'll keep my word. I need your respect if I am to live. I'm waiting for Yuri to finish his big book then I'll go and meet him. I'd like him to tell me the story of Achilles one last time. I want him to say, You see, mate, the tragic thing about Achilles is that he is the son of a mortal man and a goddess. Yuri's gruff alcoholic's voice is a comfort to me. He will tell me that the downfall of all those who aspire to immortality will be terrible. They are true public dangers. Tyrants to start with. They create a void around them, as if they had some control over death. They exterminate masses of people, and cause the imbeciles to believe that they are buying favors from the Grim Reaper: I'll give you all the corpses you like if you'll give me lifelong credit. *Nyet.* It is the revenge of Satan over God. But the masses are greater idiots than you'd think, and they prefer the God of a tyrant to a libertarian devil. Do you follow me? Even though Thetis dipped her son in the sacred fire every night, death would not spare her child altogether. Thetis was holding him by the heel, his weak spot. Moral of the story, when a mother gives birth, she kills. Now it's up to you, dumbass, to find the relationship between mothers and dictators. The correlation is blinding. Which is why everyone is blind! Get it? To tell you the truth, Vima, I don't understand

Yuri. He's too complicated for me, too much of a thinker. I wish you could get to know him, you would get along well.

I find him sprawled on his bed. He says, Above all, don't ask me for news of Achilles. He adds, Fook Achilles. And fook Solzhenitsyn. We speak English with Yuri. When he starts his day by saying fuck, relentlessly, whenever the spirit moves him, it means he's in a bad way. Very bad. It means he's having a rough time, he can't take it anymore, and don't mess with him. I don't know who Solzhenitsyn is. Yuri waves the book he's holding in his hand. Mumbles, This guy will really get you down. This guy watched his bones turn rotten in Siberia. And he dishes the rot back out to you. Shoves your nose in the putrefaction that's invisible to the naked eye. The rot in your soul and in your heart. He flings it all at you in a few words, and it works. You feel like spewing up everything you have inside, from your guts to the air in your lungs, which has turned to sulfur. Yuri has an unfortunate tendency to dwell on his obsessions. When he's in a filthy mood he always starts with Stalin's crimes. So I say to him, Fuck Stalin and all the Commanders along with him. Don't feel like talking about them. Don't feel like talking at all. Yuri gives me a sharp look. He murmurs, In the beginning there was the word. And you, dumbass Colonel, in a way, you are saying fuck the word. Maybe you're right. I'll bet you are right. I wonder if the word is not the source of all mankind's woes. It's gotta be true, you dumbass, the word drives you crazy the minute you start making sentences! You'll go bananas trying to string them together this way and that. Your questions have no valid answers. Thesis, antithesis, synthesis and you end up with fucking hypothesis. Okey-dokey, let's stick with silence, he says. It's more restful.

We spent the morning sipping vodka, in silence.

I left my studio at seven o'clock in the morning. I have to run before the appointment. Not the usual five kilometers, but ten. I have to get rid of the tension that has me in its grip. I start running and I wonder if I should let him speak, or set out my conditions from the start. I'll listen to him. But not before he answers my questions. I will say, It's my turn to interrogate you. Or I could say, Tell me everything you know about Del. Where is he? Tell me. Otherwise I'll leave. I've already been around the park four times. I still can't make up my mind. Only two more laps and I'm done. I do four. Almost fifteen kilometers instead of ten. My muscles relax at last. My mind clears. I have to let him talk. That's obvious. Listening is always preferable to talking. Let the other remove his veil, as my grandmother used to say. Give your response time to ripen.

I reach the waterfront in the port in record time. The sea, lacquered silver, stretches all the way to infinity. Fog sweeps low in whimsical gusts. A pearly web covers the warehouses and the boats. The tallest masts stab at the white monotony of the horizon. I'm early. Through the milky froth of fog rising in waves I can just make out the last café at the end of the pier. The door groans as I push it with my palm. The café is packed. Noisy. Fishermen perch on barstools and stare at the television screen set up between two beer barrels. A pudgy pink commentator is describing the major offensive of some French troops against African terrorists. His brows are knit, his voice is grave, for the circumstance. The patrons are glued to the screen. They are drinking. Sharing opinions. They get excited. Gulp down one mug of beer after the other, to the health of the Frenchies. They have to crush that horde of savages, hostage-takers. Get rid of them for us, once and for all. Of them and of their intolerant and intolerable God. I stop listening to their conversations. I absorb the background noise. I meditate on the word God. *A projection of the male desire for power, equally useful to tyrants and oligarchic democrats. A two-faced deity, one face protecting against the other face, which sows terror. Both sides are armed. Machetes, knives, sabers, and machine guns on one side, fighter planes, bombers, and drones on the other. And this side is behind the shareholders and the weapons manufacturers . . . Why does the television never speak about Africa's uranium, when that is precisely the reason why the French have gone in there . . .*

And now the television moves on to something else. As do I. They bring me my coffee. It's cold. I add sugar but don't drink it. I wait.

I have only two days left. Two days until the mission. Obviously, I won't accept. My only aim is to persuade this woman. To act as my relay. It's the only solution. She is my only possible link with you. I don't care what happens to me. I just want you to know the truth. So the children will hear it from your lips. And so I will receive justice. From you. The only judge whom I respect. The sentence of the Last Judgment will come from your lips. It doesn't matter when. I will wait for my apocalypse.

I brought Yuri's tape recorder. I'm going to record everything. It's safer that way. I'll give it to the girl. She's intelligent, your homonym. Tenacious and cautious. She's well-versed in adversity. She resisted, in Heaven. Which goes to show that if ever they start to mess with her, she'll make short work of them, whether they're cops or not. Their bullshit human rights aren't worth the paper they're written on, but she'll know how to make use of them. She knows all about waving signs with fine slogans on them. I'm going to head over there now. I want her to tell you that I've never stopped loving you. It's your love that saved me from the worst. It's all on the tape recorder. From the first dazzling gaze to the last one, which pierced my heart. I love you, my Vima. More than anything on earth.

I didn't see him come in. Nor did I sense him there behind my back. A ghost, yes, a ghost. He's lost weight. I only noticed it today. He's all muscles, made of air. No wonder he slipped past my vigilance. I only sense terrestrial beings. I can sniff them out wherever they are. I perceive them, even behind my back. But when they're made of air? I am hardly aware of them. They melt into the landscape, they go unnoticed, blend naturally into things. One does not challenge one's doubles in brotherhood.

The Colonel is taking his time. He observes the beer drinkers one by one, then the barman. It's time for the news. They're absorbed in their war again. They're taking part through the intermediary of the TV screen. The Colonel says good morning, suddenly turns around, and heads toward the door. I'll be right back, he utters over his shoulder. I follow him with my eyes. He leaves the café. Looks all around him. Is he afraid he might have been followed? Is he under surveillance? Or police protection? He comes slowly back to me. With that incomparable walk. The right foot slightly off to one side. He sits down. Orders a vodka and a strong coffee. So he drinks, bright and early. I didn't think he drank. Did he already drink back at home? In Heaven? With the torturers? In secret? After the gang rapes? What does it matter now. He empties his glass, in one go. He starts talking to me about his wife. With no other introduction.

Her name is Vima. Like me. He's crazy about her. She's magnificent. He specifies: physically, but not just that. She's unique. I reply, somewhat curtly, We are all unique. He replies, No. She's in a class on her own. Exceptional. Very intelligent. An astrophysicist. Yes indeed. He repeats indeed, *twice over. His eyes sparkle when he talks about his wife's stars and galaxies. I look at him closely and think, a high-ranking scientist has shared her life and her bed with this guy. I must look stunned. Dumbfounded. He says, as if he were reading my thoughts, I'm very proud to be her husband. The heavens hold fewer mysteries for Vima than for the Commander, who claims to represent them. The heavens belong to those who understand them. Don't you agree? You understand me, don't you? He presses the point. I don't know what to say. The Colonel goes on. He can't stop singing her praises. Piles on the superlatives. As I listen to him I wonder, distractedly, what term would most accurately express what he feels for this spouse he has praised to the skies. Pride, admiration, recognition, deference, veneration? A mixture of all of that. He breaks off to say, You wonder why I'm boring you with my wife, don't you? I nod. Intrigued. Because you're part of an equation, he explains. The formula, or more precisely the word,* equation, *makes me smile. A distant wink to his wife? I have to know that his life changed dramatically because of me, bait 455. He corrects himself, Not because of, but perhaps thanks to you. He speaks clearly, without stopping to breathe. He pauses, then goes on to recount in great detail that winter evening when his wife Vima discovered the CD containing my interrogation. A torture session. The penultimate one. These facts, which he kept secret, make up the piece of the puzzle that was missing from his declarations to the Office. I have a better understanding now of his absolute discretion regarding his family. The freedom Vima the spouse demanded for Vima in Heaven would cost the former her life if ever They found out. She still lives back there. In the jaws of the lion. Again the Colonel says, I'm worried about my wife. He has instinctively lowered his voice, and he's sweating profusely. I know it so well, that unreasonable, atavistic fear. We are speaking our language. We do not exist for those morons in the bar. They bellow, they're getting drunk, not paying the slightest attention to anything around them. And yet. We are spying on them. Both of us. Our furtive gazes meet briefly. The Colonel pauses for a moment. He is at a loss for words, as he evokes the first and last lovers' quarrel in his life. He would like to forget everything. His wife's ultimatum. The pain of departure. The dizziness of exile. The years of futile hope. He falls silent. Suddenly. Drained. Exhausted.*

I order two more coffees. And a double vodka, he says to the waiter, in a weak voice. I let the silence and the vodka take effect. Then I ask him the question I was bound to ask: Am I in his debt? No, he replies. I do not owe him anything, in any case. He adds, In a way I'm the one who is in your debt. Is his wife in danger? He hopes not. He made arrangements before he fled. She has been repudiated. She has had nothing to do with the traitor, the fugitive. She was interrogated. Exonerated. He says, She's strong, a tough character, like you. And for once the Colonel blesses the power granted to man thanks to the reign of God. I say, All you had to do was snap your fingers and you were divorced! He looks at me, startled. He laughs. I smile. The atmosphere becomes more relaxed. It does us good, both of us. He says, But you know, you can never be sure of anything in the Theological Republic! What does he want from me? He wants me to write. He says it again, intensely, Yes, write. I say nothing. He says, I read you, I had to. I pause to think. Oh, yes, he must have read the draft of my novel. The only personal text I did not burn, and which they confiscated along with all the rest when Del was arrested. A few pages of a great love story. Left hanging. Or maybe he read only the little tales about the djinns which I made up for the guard in Heaven. In any case he thinks I owe him this favor! Caught off guard, now it's my turn to be at a loss for words. His request is so strange. Abrupt. What am I supposed to write? What his wife needs to know. He is afraid. Afraid he may never see her again. Even if the Office decides to grant him his papers at last, she could only join him after a year has gone by. He is sick, he has to have an operation. The doctors . . . I stop listening. I don't believe him. He's lying. It's pathetic. I know he is. He knows that I know. He's in fine shape. But he's afraid. His fear is palpable. Illness is just a pretext. If the Commander's services find him, they will kill him. For sure. That's what he's afraid of. I have to ask him. I hesitate. Think better of it. He won't answer. No point wasting my breath. But it disturbs me. To know he is hunted, the way I was, the way Del and his friends were—it upsets me. Hunted, that's what the entire country is. Now the Colonel is one of the hunted. He has been reinstated as a citizen. We have become full-fledged compatriots. But what about the past? Can you just erase it with a swipe of your hand? And that pool of putrefaction he waded into, without blinking an eyelid? The stench of it? The blood spilled before his eyes, the urine and cum the captives were forced to swallow, and he didn't lift a finger? The deep reason for my empathy is not politically correct. It is the lover in him who has disarmed me, inspired me, impressed me. The feelings which animate him make me think of Del. My beautiful love. He should tell me about him now. But I remain silent. I ask nothing. My lips are sealed. Like in Heaven. I'm afraid of what I might find out.

Anger washes over me. I'm being ridiculous. The Colonel is not Del. They have nothing in common. I hate this man. I must hate him. What would he have done if they had taken his own wife as bait? No, I don't want to forget who you are. How can a shitface like you lay claim to my understanding? I look at him. His eyes are veiled. His gaze is unbearably gentle. Which only kindles my rage. He is imploring me. Do this for my wife, who saved you. And suddenly the truth explodes before my eyes. I feel the shame burning my cheeks. I feel the implacable sting of jealousy inflame my being right to the roots of my hair. I am jealous of this Vima. Jealous of the love this reformed assassin feels for her. With his gentle eyes. Indeed, Del is not the Colonel. Did he ever love me? The sensitive spouse. The sublime man. The literary friend. Refined. The adored one, who abandoned me. Perhaps it is the same as the tenuous link between love and torture. Torture, like love, destroys, distorts, and transforms. Indubitably. Love, like torture, alters bodies. From precipices of torment. Both love and torture mortify the soul deep in one's inner chaos. Where the self disintegrates. Driven to such an extreme, a monster is transformed into a man of conscience, and an idealist into a turncoat. Where is Del in this equation? Where am I, actually? Repulsion. Compassion. Toward Del. Toward the Colonel. Toward myself. Feelings that pull me this way and that. Men whom I confuse and who confuse me. I feel my heart leaping from my chest. And the pain is stifling me. In a hoarse voice I say, I don't write anymore. I don't want to write anymore. The Colonel seems desperate. His voice grows hard. There are sparks in his gaze. He says, You owe us your life. You can't abandon us. I feel a vise closing around me. I am propelled back to Heaven. Torturers, rape, blows, spit, insults, and then deliverance, the moment the man sitting opposite me snaps his fingers, after so many years of mystery. He is right, I have to agree. Those who have known the suffering that is Heaven can no longer prevaricate. I cannot, must not say no to him. I say, I need some time. I have to think about it. He replies that there is no time. The man believes he is doomed. Now I'm convinced. I say nothing more. I've already agreed. I look at him, and blink. All right, I'll do it.

He takes a little tape recorder from his pocket and puts it on the table in front of me. It's all here. Above all, don't lose it. It's the only copy. He's embarrassed. He stammers, It's a bit repetitive, a bit muddled, but it's clean. There are no lies, only the truth. Clean, a word that addicts use, which goes to show how dependent this man truly is. The Colonel coughs, brings me back to his presence. I'll let you finalize this for Vima, he says. You'll do it, won't you? I blink, but I don't say I'll do it. He gets up. He has to go. I say, Wait a minute. He changes his mind. Sits back down. My voice runs away with me. Where is Del? Where and when did he get the note to you, telling me to leave? Where is he? Where is my husband? I repeat my question, stupidly, for fear I might burst into tears. The only answer I need from him is to hear him say, He didn't betray you. Del isn't a stool pigeon. I would like him to swear that to me. And then for him to assure me that Del is going to come and be with me. That it's only a question of time. A few weeks. A few months at the most. I feel my throat swelling. My tears are flowing, drowning me. He says, It was a long time ago, I don't remember the exact date, then he stops in the middle of his sentence. He's run out of inspiration. I can hear the temptation to lie in his hesitation, his breathlessness.

I had been waiting for that moment right from the start of our meeting. I had prepared myself for it. A smooth explanation. The standard phrases. And now I feel stupid, at a loss. I don't know what to reply. A lie that offers relief: is it ever justified? A pathetic dilemma. I give it some thought, then say simply, Everything he did was because he hoped to save you. This answer, which has come from my conscience, is neither a lie nor the truth. Just a possibility. Because no one other than Del himself will ever know whether he sold his comrades. And if he did, did he do it before his wife's arrest or after? Did he try in vain to obtain a safe-conduct for her? The mystery will remain intact. There have been hundreds of arrests in recent years. There has never been any coordination between different prisons or even between different sections of the same prison. The authorities went berserk whenever anyone escaped, with the ensuing chaos and panic. And their rage was becoming counterproductive. They acted in a compulsive, paranoid manner. It became common practice to kidnap baits and hold them in reserve, just in case, then torture and eliminate them the moment they became a burden. The machine had gotten out of control and was operating in a closed circuit.

No one seemed to know how to stop the hemorrhage. Under these conditions, how was anyone supposed to know when or why Del might have betrayed his comrades? I look at her and say again, with conviction, Whatever he did, it was for you. She says nothing. She doesn't believe me. She is weeping. In silence. Quietly. Not making a scene. Not a single feature on her face has changed. A marble statue, a cascade of tears. No doubt this was how she found relief in Heaven. Beneath her hood stinking of filth and hatred. I say to her, I am convinced of this, and I tell her about my meeting with Del. I dwell on the last few minutes. How he hurried to catch up with me to add their coded word at the end of the letter. To be sure she would leave. So she would be safe. So she— She interrupts me. Runs her hands over her face. Wipes away her tears. Mutters, Safe? Says the word over and over as if she doesn't understand what it means. Safe? Safe? She is gasping. And where is he? Wasn't he supposed to join me? He didn't keep his promise. Why? You must know! How can I tell her that I know nothing? Or that I don't know enough, or that I know too much to be able to speak about it? That it would be better not to disclose convictions that are not necessarily justified, but which undoubtedly would cause irreparable hurt? How can I tell her that a man who fails to accomplish his dreams will be driven to renounce them? That it is himself he abandons, not others. I could go on about this topic for hours. I know a thing or two about it, after all. But how could I tell her that the worst betrayal is to one's own self? I don't have the courage to say, Vima, this burden is too heavy. One has to be alone to bear it. Far from the gazes of others. How can I make her understand that a man who is marked by guilt cannot confront a woman to whom he has caused so much suffering. What right does he have? To hold forth about such things would be as useless as it is indecent. Truth which causes pain loses its truthfulness. And besides, what do I really know? I'm merely trying to compromise as best I can. I'm wasting my breath. She asks me, Is he all right? I think about her husband, how decrepit he had become, old before his time, and I reply, He's all right, Vima, as well as can be expected. Not a word, obviously, about the little boy I saw in the rearview mirror. The little boy he had with another woman. I go on, He isn't . . . he'll never be the man you knew, ever again. But he will love you all his life. No one can take from you what you had together. Your salvation is his. If you begin to enjoy life again, he too will live a bit better. He will feel it, he's bound to, instinctively. She looks at me. Takes my hand. The contact of her skin is like a flame, burning me inside. This is the first time a woman has taken my hand in all the time I've been in exile. Five years.

He is speaking. I can feel my tears burning on my cheeks. He says safe. *That Del wanted to keep me safe. What is this madman talking about? Can I ever be safe without the refuge of his gaze? Without his embrace? And his hands on my forehead, calming my headaches. The slump in my shoulders vanishes instantly with the touch of his palms, the concentrated tenderness in his fingertips. Safe? What is this* safe *he is talking about? Del's love was what kept me safe. More than anything, when I was in the depths of hell. How dare he utter this word so lightly? He smiles. Rubs his moist eyes. Tries to explain the inexplicable. Comes out with things that are so banal they horrify me. He speaks to me the way you would speak to a child. Gently, and with conviction. A little more and he would dry my tears and blow my nose. I don't know how or why—to shut him up, probably—I place my hand on his. It's cold. Slightly damp. He goes tense. As if he'd received an electric shock. I wrap my fingers around his. Squeeze them. Dig my nails into his flesh. What is the matter with me? Perhaps it's a desire, no, a visceral need to seal the pact that binds me to this man. To silence him so he hears only the voice of the heart. Be quiet. You don't believe any more than I do in the honeyed words you've been coming out with, halfheartedly. At the banquet of the fallen queen, formulas like what-we've-been-through and he-will-love-you-all-his-life, the insipid treacle you've been dishing up as your main course, well, they won't go down well. Even with your shots of vodka, down in one. Bullshit, dear Colonel. There is no remedy that can cause the wound to close. It remains open. Whether I owe my life to you or to your wife does not figure in our equation, as you put it. It's not a savior I see in you but my brother in suffering. Hounded by the sorrow of love. That's what it's all about, and nothing else.*

The Colonel is stunned. My grip has stopped him in his tracks. I'm aware of that. I can feel it. I can feel the beating of his veins beneath my palm. I am holding him with the tension of my being concentrated in my fingers of bronze. I could crush him. With his free hand he taps my wrist, awkwardly. He would like to withdraw his hand. It's pathetic, the way his fingers tap before they let go. His arm dangles uselessly by his side and he slumps forward. If I don't let him go, his heart will. And then our pain, our twice-felt pain, will explode in our faces and blow us to bits. I loosen my fingers and free him. My palm is burning. His palm has been branded. The blood coagulates around the imprint of my nails. He rises slowly to his feet. Looks at me. I put the tape recorder into my bag. That was the answer he was waiting for. He says thank you, and turns on his heel.

A man with a lopsided walk, wearing a worn overcoat, moves away down the pier. Briefly caught in a pale ray of sunlight. Then the figure vanishes. I never asked him his name. Nor do I remember his case number at the Office. The curtain falls on the strange encounter between the bait and the Colonel. All that remains now is a tape recorder and a promise. From him to his Vima. From Vima to her Del.

I walk home. I take a steaming bath then a restorative cold shower. The cold water unravels my tangled nerves, helps me think. Should I listen to the cassette in one go, or in short spells? Shouldn't I begin with the end? With my escape and . . . Maybe he even talks about Del. Maybe he says everything he couldn't or wouldn't tell me in person. No, I mustn't shoot ahead. I have to begin with the beginning. I have to . . . I let the cold water run over me. I massage my legs, and rub the tight muscles in my back by twisting around the way I used to in Heaven. I'll begin with the beginning. And take my time. The time it takes.

I've been listening to the Colonel for half an hour. The tape lasts three and a half hours. I'm only at the very beginning of the story.

"I had just turned eighteen, a young volunteer on leave . . ." I could hear him and see him. He was young, handsome. More handsome than an hour ago when I left him. A fine head, sculpted in angles. Prominent cheekbones. Big dark eyes—not the least bit protruding—just somewhat deep-set. Which added mystery to his charm. An athlete's body, long and slender. I close my eyes. I remove the headphones. The loudspeaker continues to broadcast the Colonel's words. The echo amplifies his voice. The love song of the man who snapped his fingers spreads through me. I incorporate him, bit by bit. Several times over, this man who loves the other Vima says, "I may be a murderer but I am madly in love. Don't forget that. You have to tell my story from that angle." And I find him moving, in more ways than one, this

murderer who is madly in love. Because of the simplicity of his words, where there are no adjectives, no superlatives, no emphasis. A visceral love in all its clarity. The Colonel goes straight to the point. The story is linear. The episodes of his life are told in chronological order. He avoids commentary, ponderousness, useless details. He doesn't go on and on. Doesn't tire his listener. Describes situations clearly. Speaks quickly. Uses everyday words. Prefers short sentences. Five to describe their meeting. "I met her at a wedding. It was at the beginning of the war. I was a young volunteer on leave. I came late to the party. She was sitting next to the bride and I saw no one else." And three to describe how he fell, head over heels. "She was so young. Scarcely fifteen and already a woman. The love of my life and no one else's." Four about the obstacles to their marriage. "My eldest brother, who had been head of the family since our father died, was a fanatic of the new regime and he didn't trust Vima. She didn't wear the uniform the government had imposed. Vima's father was suspected of being ideologically soft, well-disposed toward the former regime, so he was also under suspicion. My brother forbade our union."

From that faraway province of a country in turmoil, the young volunteer returned to the front with the woman of his dreams in his heart. A year and a half later he would make her his bride. His lifelong companion had her eyes on the sky and her head on her shoulders. A young woman who set down her conditions before marriage. His first private conversation with Vima is described in sober terms. I would even say gravely. The young volunteer was under her spell; now he said he was ready to confront his family if his lovely lady— The young woman did not let him finish his sentence. She was one step ahead of him, but she would be setting the rules. She was prepared to marry him. "It was a shock," says the Colonel. He had never heard a young girl speak with so much self-confidence. I can hear the irony in his tired voice. The self-mockery. Of the mature man vis-à-vis the young soldier, a believer, whose convictions would be shaken by an adolescent—"a young girl" he says, several times over. The warrior prepared to sacrifice his life for the leader who inflamed spirits: now he was in awe of a tiny, dauntless woman. He had to react, to look composed. And why was she prepared to marry him? Did she already love him? Vima laughed. Her laughter was candid. Instantaneous. Enchanting. She said, Love? That's a big word. Do you think you love me? I think you're handsome. I fancy you. A great deal, even. But I want to go on with my studies. No matter what. Nothing is easy for girls. Especially in the provinces. He was completely disorientated. She had dazzled him with her boldness. Her frankness. Her obsessions. Vima's father didn't have the means to send her to the capital where she could have continued her studies at a private school. She would love the man who allowed her to fulfill her dream. To study. Completing her studies was her reason for living. She didn't mention the Commander, whom the young soldier so admired. She didn't like him. The old man hated people who used their minds. He hated women. And he fuelled the hatred of provincial despots toward those who did the work of the devil. But not a word. No opening her heart to someone whose belief in the leader was unconditional. Blind. Deaf. The potential fiancé was absolutely convinced that the holy man was misunderstood, poorly informed, surrounded by the wrong people. She left him to his imaginings. She merely spoke to him about her passion for the heavens. Not the Commander's heavens, which were the habitat of his God. But the heavens of mathematicians and physicists . . .

I find it difficult to picture this unusual, provincial young woman in the feverish atmosphere of the early days of the holy revolution. The Commander had infused people's spirits with a mystico-political passion. The diktats of the new father of the nation were a great success. The war against the external enemy justified the internal repression. Protesters were brought to heel or eliminated. True citizens were those who were behind the

Commander. It was impossible to escape from him. To ignore him. Vima was an exception. "She was special," said the Colonel. She wasn't interested in politics. Even less so in the war. Bombing. Hardship. Revolutionary violence. Everything that made up the everyday life of other people. It was as if nothing really affected her. Didn't she live in the same country? When he asked her this, she invariably replied, What good does it do to keep talking about misfortune? And besides, the moment you looked above you there was no more misfortune. Another place—the sky, its vastness, its fabulous mysteries—had taken over her life. She was enchanted. The stars were closer to her than human beings were. She had been living among the stars since childhood. They conspired with her, and she wanted to unveil their secrets. The brilliant proof of the way life was perpetually evolving. Food for thought for an entire lifetime. How could she fail to escape from all the rest? To remove herself from anything superfluous, thanks to mathematical abstraction and its relative truths? The soldier was flabbergasted. Again and again I listen to the passages where he speaks for her. And eventually above the Colonel's monotonous voice I hear Vima. I can feel her presence.

Who are you, Vima? A dreamer? I don't think so. Or at least not in the commonly accepted meaning of the word. You have your head in the stars but your feet are on the ground. You know what you want. You are demanding. And you get what you want. Everything began with the promises of a shared desire. You made them unequivocally clear. Your suitor was handsome, you fancied him, and you told him so. There is nothing more thrilling, for a man who is hopelessly in love. But even then your mind was ahead of your feelings. The ultimate condition for marriage was for love to be kept under control. Which the young man found deeply disturbing. Even today these recollections confuse your husband's grieving memory. The Colonel falters when the time comes to speak of the most extravagant clause in your marriage contract. He says, "When Vima . . ." And stops. Starts again: "I don't remember when Vima . . ." Coughs. Goes on in a changed voice: "Vima told me, literally: You must know that I don't want any children until I've finished my studies." You were only fifteen years old. How could a mischievous young girl, as he put it, possibly see so far ahead? You might say it was your stars. You had an acute awareness of distances measured in light-years. It reduced your suitor to silence. The Colonel admits as much, without shame. "I said nothing for a moment. But I agreed. Of course I did. I thought, foolishly, that the baccalaureate would be enough for her, the end to studies for a married woman . . ."

The young volunteer, with his war medals, promoted to Captain, married Vima in secret, a little over a year after they first met. His family had nothing more to say in the matter, and they would never know the terms of the marriage contract which Vima had required, in due form. She obtained her baccalaureate in science, with a citation for excellence, and without affiliation to any school, thanks to the intervention of her military husband. Because there could be no mixing of the sexes, women were barred from the scientific departments at provincial universities, so she took the degree course in mathematics and physics under the supervision of former university professors who had been forced to retire. She also learned English, in the utmost secrecy. The provincial rulers frowned on those who spoke the language of the devil. Vima would rather converse with educated demons from the West than with local primates, she said. She was preparing for the future. Thinking about her higher education. She would obtain her Ph.D. abroad, or else by correspondence. She drew up a list of the best science universities in the West. With the utmost discretion, she gradually unveiled her plans. "Everything in its own time," says the Colonel, without elaborating. The fact remains that she spoke English fluently by the time her husband, steadily rising in the ranks, was transferred to the capital. Six months later, one of the private universities opened a science department reserved for women. Vima obtained her Bachelor's degree in less than a year. And embarked on a Master's in physics.

Only once did the Colonel allow himself to wax lyrical. No doubt he was hoping to communicate to me, and I quote, "my dazzling Vima's capacity for wonder, which I found truly enchanting!" He was sober once again when speaking of the end of the war. A futile, treacherous, lethal war, which left one million dead, including dozens of his friends. He was twenty-seven years old. She was twenty-three. They still had no children. Since he was keeping his promise. As the pill was not allowed, when she was ovulating he did not touch her. For fear he would not be able to control himself. He knew she would have an abortion, if ever . . . She had told him as much, without the slightest remorse. He kept his chin up, even when it meant putting up with his family's insults. They said he was impotent. That she was barren. The young career officer's sorrows and fears occasionally color his story. He was frightened. For both of them. Above all for her. People didn't like his Vima. They said wicked things about her. Those who were close to him—by blood, in spirit—denigrated her. And felt sorry for him. The captain was well thought of in the Army and by the Commander, but he had a weak spot, and that would be his perdition, said his loyal followers, his only confidants and companions at the front. They owed him their lives. So he owed them his attention. They could see that Vima was his weakness. The Colonel's Achilles' heel was his wife. An Achilles' heel who had not given him a child. A woman who hung around universities for no good reason was bound to be sick. She was suspected of every flaw. Those who were real men hated his wife and treated him with scorn. His superior officers told him, Soft guy, soft husband; soft husband, cheating wife. And all this without anyone even knowing that she didn't pray. That she didn't believe in all their hogwash. They would both be good for the gallows if anyone overheard the way she spoke about the Commander. Vima was beautiful. And she knew it. She was a flirt, and did not respect the modest dress code. No one ever saw her wearing the dark uniform that covered respectable women from head to foot. Officials' wives singled her out for criticism. It was pointless to warn her of her dangerous behavior, pointless to ask her to make an effort: Vima the rebel just dug her heels in. She would listen to no one except her own conscience. That was the situation. Their nights of love effaced everything, dissolved fear and doubt. He could forget about his family, his superiors, the Commander, all the rules in force, the laws of the theological Republic. Summer was a good time for them to prolong their escapades and sleepless nights. The young soldier had certain privileges, including that of camping wherever he wanted whenever he wanted. The desert was their favorite place. All alone on earth, in the middle of nowhere, they were free to explore their romance in an otherworldly absence of constraint. It was there, with all the stars within reach, that Vima was happiest. It was there that she subjugated him beyond his senses. Her intelligence, her knowledge, her insatiable curiosity humbled him. She transformed him, from mere flesh into spirit. At this point the Colonel's voice trembles. He so loved the constellations, the way Vima described them to him. Did he know, she asked, that the Milky Way, the expanding galaxy, contained hundreds of billions of stars? That its diameter was in the region of a hundred thousand light-years? The young officer's Eve stood naked before him, unique on earth, pointing to the canopy of heaven and shouting at the top of her lungs, This is what I worship. My God is nothing but concentrated intelligence, a supermassive black hole. The cosmos or the complexity of order born from chaos. Which surpasses us, but which is not inaccessible. Not at all. The paths to my God are not impenetrable. Science is his only Law. How do you expect me to pray to a God who is ignorant, vindictive, jealous, spiteful, bad-tempered, ugly, and as stupid as they come, forged in the image of those who claim to represent him? The representatives of my

God are the likes of Galileo, Omar Khayyám, Einstein. Do you understand?

The birth of their daughter—whom she called Urania, to her mother-in-law's great displeasure—came at the end of Vima's first academic cycle. She had obtained her Master's in applied physics. Her husband and her family all thought that now at last she would begin to focus on her home and her child. While expecting the second one. Since the husband was not impotent. Any more than she was barren. The first duty of a wife was to provide her husband with an heir. A daughter didn't count. The leaders did not take the sacred duties of a mother lightly. Were they not a woman's purpose in life? That was what the Commander said, again and again, whenever the issue of a man's other half came up. Later, much later, Vima might eventually teach at the female university. "And do you know what?" adds the Colonel with a laugh. Which goes on for a moment. Filling the room and making me laugh in turn. "Vima," he says in a joyful voice, "found an accomplice who surpassed herself. My old sister. A war widow. Who had no children." After the birth Vima stayed in bed. And entrusted the baby to her sister-in-law, who was crazy about the little girl. Naturally the old woman had every good reason to defend the young mother's cause. The child would lack for nothing. Vima could continue her studies. She submitted her application to study for a doctorate by correspondence to one of the best universities in Europe. She was immediately accepted. Thanks to her husband, she also obtained the right to use the Army's observatory, with the powerful telescopes she needed for her research. It was at this time that her high-ranking officer husband's problems began; he had just been promoted to Colonel. Now to me he says, "I'm not going to bore you by repeating what is contained in my file. You know all, or almost all, the ins and outs of my career. You translated my deposition. Except that I didn't say anything about the tension in my family due to my work. Vima wanted me to resign. She was putting pressure on me. When did they start, the lies that turned me into the traitor she eventually unmasked? Was it that winter when I swore I would resign? Or in spring when I showed her my real fake letter of resignation? Or more precisely, was it the day when, proud as a peacock, I led her triumphantly into my magnificent businessman's office? There I was, the Commander's Army Intelligence liaison officer, in the pay of the Residence! Our son had just been born. Vima was busy with her research for her doctoral dissertation. I was living on standby. Between heaven and hell. Acutely aware of the usurper in me who sooner or later would be banished from Eden to Gehenna for good. Without passing through purgatory. I don't know, without betraying myself, how to explain the deeper reasons for my behavior. Panic, cowardice, the lure of personal gain, or quite simply indifference? When you are not personally affected by barbarity, it becomes so banal as to anesthetize you. This is a terrible thing to acknowledge. But it is what I experienced. The system was total, absolute, unfailing. Otherwise, armed with the innocence of distance, I would never have been able to watch those filmed sessions of the torture inflicted on political prisoners. The CD of bait 455 'to be examined'—that is the term used by the authorities, to be exact—was not the first of its kind. As you can imagine."

There is a slight hissing and crackling for a few seconds, then the Colonel goes on to relate the events of the night when bait 455 suddenly came into his life. He says, "For a person like me who believes in signs, Number 455's first name was a sign. The detonator of an imminent downfall." He spares no details. He lists all the errors he committed. Number one: he took the CD home. Number two: he watched it on his personal laptop, which he left out in plain sight on the table in the living room. Number three: he didn't switch the computer off. Number four: he didn't put the CD away. "You'd have to be stupid," he admits, "not to realize that these mistakes were made deliberately. Subconsciously, but a long time in advance." He wanted, he says, to put an end to all the lying. And to all the internalized violence, gnawing away at him from within. He then describes in detail the night Vima accused him. How his spouse rescued him from drowning, at the last minute, then sent him away from the house. And he adds this detail: "Vima, too, was going to move away. She didn't want to live in that house anymore, the house that had belonged to the ruined doctor. She said the villa was ruined, the way the country was, and to live together with the usurpers was to approve of them. We had to leave everything behind . . . First me, then her." His voice cracks, trembles. The Colonel admits that Vima did not save me out of love. My death would have been too easy, and still equally pointless. I had to undo the harm. I had to save you. Now I learn, from the lips of the man who, with a snap of his fingers, removed me from the clutches of the criminals in maximum security Section 209, every step of how I escaped. He refers to his atonement in a strange way. He says, "It was astonishing, how she recovered, that human wreck I entrusted to the doctors at the military hospital." The human wreck was me. He says this, not the least bit embarrassed, in a neutral tone of voice. As if it were about some third person. A stranger to me. He says, "After only one week in intensive care, Number 455 looked human again. I gazed at her as she slept. She was peaceful. Incredibly relaxed. And beautiful. With a childlike beauty. So fragile, the freshness of youth regained. Nothing obtuse about her face, with its regular features and delicate lines. Nothing in her physiognomy—that of the good little girl—to suggest such an obstinate nature. Her will had been tempered by steel." I find it difficult to withhold my tears when he describes his conversations with my mother. He says, "The old lady's voice petrified me. Her grief was unbearable. It was intolerable, the hope she placed in me. She called me her savior. The murderer had been sanctified. According to the old lady, I was proof of God's existence. The God her daughter did not believe in would save her, thanks to one of his angels: me."

I listen as the Colonel recounts my mother's confidences about my father's death. And I hear myself screaming, Nooooo, *in my cell, under my burlap bag, I hear them saying, Your old man has kicked the bucket. Because of you, filthy whore. You and your bastard husband. This* nooooo *pounds in my head while the Colonel's voice, not without emotion, describes my mother's sorrow. She said to him, My husband adored Vima. After she disappeared he went around all the prisons, the hospitals, the morgues. Hundreds of times. Months of useless searching. One fine day some strangers called us on the telephone to tell us that our daughter was imprisoned in the maximum security section, in solitary confinement, without visiting rights. My husband's heart gave way. He collapsed. We had difficulty removing the receiver from his hand. The Colonel clears his throat. He says, "Vima's mother thinks that her husband's soul is finally at rest, thanks to me. The day before their escape, which came about through my good offices, she said to me, as a sort of goodbye, Until my dying day I will pray for you, for your happiness . . . My happiness! Tell your mother, if ever you decide to tell her about our meeting, that she was the one who gave me my last glimmers of happiness. Thank her for me." The Colonel doesn't say anything about his own escape, which has been recorded in his deposition at the Office. Not a word about his parting with his family. No emotional outpourings. Nothing about how torn he must have been. Or about the vertigo of exile. His hopes betrayed. He must have thought, 455 knows all this by heart.*

"Don't try to reach me," he insists at the end of the tape. "I'll get in touch with you." His last words follow, unsteadily. He says, "In keeping with the wishes of the love of my life, my soul has been restored to me, thanks to her namesake. Vima, a blessed name which I venerate, for everything in it that is now holy." He also says, "455, I am not asking you for forgiveness. You must not give it to me. Under any pretext. I want my wife to forgive me. But not you. In that way, both of you will render justice. And in that way, other reluctant murderers will be unmasked." I don't

follow his logic or what he hopes to gain. But to hear him call me 455 makes me tremble. The boundary between the two Vimas is perfectly clear.

It is late at night. I'm exhausted. But I listen to the Colonel, over and over, ad nauseam. And one question is preying on my mind. Did Del ever love me the way this man loves his Vima?

Before going back to the detention center I make a long detour. I stop at all the bars in the port. I drink three more shots of vodka, one after the other. They don't do much to get me warm. Make me feel a bit lighter. I was hoping for calm but in fact I'm exhausted. She will do what it takes. I'm sure of it. She will find you, and fill you in, my Vima. You will know what you need to know, if I were to disappear . . . I know I'll be risking a lot if I turn down their scheme. In Intelligence there is no going back. No more here than back there. It's an international law. I wasn't naïve and I didn't trust them. I tried my luck, I didn't really have any choice. You say we always have a choice. And no doubt you are right. The proof is that I won't accept their mission. They think they've got me. They say, This guy will do anything to be reunited with his wife and children. Yes, I would accept my own damnation to be reunited with you. But those idiots don't know you. They don't know that I would never be reunited with you if I went back to working as an assassin. Fuck their mission, as Yuri would say. You can rest assured, I won't lift a finger. Deep down I still have some hope, in spite of my fears. Maybe they'll leave me alone. I'll put it in writing, everything I couldn't tell your namesake. My testament as a free man, if you like. Beginning with my incestuous relations with the Western intelligence agencies. I know what I have to do for my letter to reach the appropriate quarters. That doesn't worry me. I wasn't born yesterday. Once it's all in writing, I'll go and find them.

And I'll say *nyet*, like Yuri. I'm staying indoors. My field of operation is this office, these computer screens and boxes of archives. It was in our contract. As soon as I say that, I'll be good for quarantine. They'll take away the few rights they had granted me up to now. I'll be under house arrest and transferred to the center for undesirable asylum-seekers. No more freedom of movement until further notice. No more right to communicate however I see fit. Yuri and all the other inmates at the detention center will be interrogated and briefed. A cop with a dejected expression will inform them that their former co-detainee was a plant working on behalf of an enemy government. A spy. A filthy snitch who rats on the nationals of his country of origin. They'll ignore me, they'll let me stew for a while. Will they give me a second chance? Will they come back to see me? Only if they think I'm worth it. I'm the first to have my doubts. Serious doubts. A man with an Achilles' heel is prone to sudden U-turns. Weakness is fatal in this profession. Once you've let someone down, it's a slippery slope. A first screwup leads to a second, and then to a third. No, I've become worthless. There will be reprisals. All that remains is to find out when, how, and in what order. Enough. Let's move on to something else. I'll take you out this evening, my Vima. We'll celebrate. Just the two of us, gorgeous. I've been thinking about you so much. You will be here, more than ever. I bought myself a fine suit. I chose one that's just your taste. Yuri couldn't believe his eyes when he saw the pictures of me in a suit, superb! You look like 007, you dumbass. Is she the one who dressed you up like Bond? Indeed, Yuri, I was the only high-ranking officer in the Commander's army who wore tailor-made suits. Ah, you are as elegant as a queen, my Vima. You have the wisdom of a goddess. I would need Yuri's gift of the gab to describe you the way you deserve to be described. The honor of being your man is no small matter. You may have noticed how I often walk behind you. It's normal. One must behave humbly in the presence of the goddess of heavenly knowledge, who knows all the secrets of all that is infinitely on high. You object. You don't want to hear me talking like those assholes who drive us to distraction with their fucking phantasmagorical sky. All right. Let me amend that: you know that you know nothing. Just an infinitesimal part of the mysteries of the universe. Satisfied? Good. Yes, we will celebrate tonight. Together. We'll drink to your health. Your health. I've been saving. My pockets are full of cash. More than enough to spend an unforgettable evening at whatever passes for a swanky restaurant in this town. I am ready, my Vima.

The letters have been signed and dated. I am dressed to the nines. And you are pretty as a picture. Your dress, the color of the setting sun, looks ravishing on you. You are magnificent. The sparkle of your honeyed eyes makes me melt. I'm sick with longing for you. Why not invite Yuri? Ah, Vima, you have always known how to change the subject when my emotions run away with me. Of course. I will ask the *poète maudit* to accompany us. Yes, that's an excellent idea. But he'll have to dress up, too. No way is he wearing his grunge jeans and his vindictive proletarian plaid shirt. He has to be an honor to you. To deserve you. In the time it takes him to change, I'll put the letters somewhere safe. In their cenotaph. We'll go and dine all three of us at the Imperial, the grandest restaurant in town. On television they call it a hangout for jet-setters and princesses! Then we'll go on a bar crawl. You've never drunk a drop of alcohol in your life, but you'll be a match for Yuri. For sure. Down the hatch, my Vima. Down the hatch. Don't forget, I love you.

No news from the Colonel. Two weeks have gone by since our meeting. I check my answering machine every day. From wherever I am. I keep an eye on my inbox. Morning and evening. Nothing. Complete silence. I've just finished transcribing the cassette. I cleaned it up. The way he asked me to. I would like to tell him about my project. To thank him for having restored my pleasure in writing. I thought I would be incapable of stringing two words together. Now all I can think about is this book. The book of intersecting promises. The Colonel's promise to his wife. My promise to Del. Or rather, the book of the intersecting pledges; my pledge to Del. The person I love without knowing why. The book of scarred loves. Dedicated to the person who destroyed the soul of Number 455. A message tossed into the wind. Del, why did you forsake me?

I have spent a week drawing up an outline for the book. And another week looking for titles. I've chosen three from out of a dozen. The Lovesick Murderer. The Man Who Snapped his Fingers. The Colonel and Bait 455. *I have formatted the titles and the synopsis, and I've called a young fashionable editor, Lars Gunar. The friend of a friend. The only thing he has read of mine is one short story in translation, which appeared in a literary journal not long after I arrived here. He's interested in my life. All I have to do is get started. He'll take care of the rest. He's definitely interested. Lars is not surprised to hear from me. He was expecting my call, or so he says. What would he say to a love story? A wild, intense, improbable love. After a few moments' hesitation he replies, Your love story, without the political dimension—I interrupt him. I put him right, it's not my story. But the passion of a former colonel in the Theological Republic for a high-flying scientist. The man was involved in crimes committed by the regime. And the lover . . . I break off. I'll send him a synopsis. Before hanging up Lars asks, Why are you starting with someone else's story and not your own? What I feel like saying is, Mine has been aborted, left hanging. I mumble something about a promise, a tribute to a free woman who has refused to bow down. A mirror effect? he asks. I suddenly fall silent. I am overwhelmed by Del, my heartbreaker. And I hang up.*

I hope to hear from the Colonel. Tomorrow means a fresh start, a new promise.

For the last twenty days I've been in the detention center for illegal migrants. A place where any hope of freedom is gone. Possible freedom. Potential. Hypothetical. The walls ooze with the anxiety of depressive insomniacs. The pestilential rejects of humanity, waiting to be extradited. A factory for the despondent. Men in the prime of life, twiddling their thumbs. Morning to night. The hardiest among them rebel. Shout their rage, after midnight. They won't put up with it, they say. They'll fight. They know how to defend themselves . . . The most courageous among them make plans for a possible future. They get excited. Pass around a bottle of adulterated vodka. Drown themselves in it, and forget the pale nights. To hear them, you'd think all you have to do is set sail for England and El Dorado. There are honest people-smugglers . . . you just have to find them. A few hours spent brushing aside the bad news of the day. They have put aside the thoughts of their mates' corpses, mates who set out on the rotting crafts of slave-ship smugglers. They thought they were honest, too.

I hear shouting in the corridor. I won't get involved. I drift off. I am lulled by the murmur of hushed conversation. I ferment my nightmares. I miss Yuri and his stories. I tell myself I should have gone on waiting for Godot, the way he told me to, instead of venturing into the labyrinth of the secret services. Dens of spies, not something I would recommend, he used to say. Godot was the last story Yuri told me. Tonight I prefer it to the one about Achilles. I too dream of the future's probabilities.

I could slip on the part of Godot, and you'd be waiting for me, my Vima. Just one hour with you, time enough to tell you one of Yuri's stories. To impress you. To dazzle you with all the things I've learned while we've been apart. To make love to you as if it were a fairy tale unfolding. For years you took me traveling in your Milky Way, tucked inside the sparkling Big Dipper. I wish I could tell you about the feats of Achilles. My desperate, absurd waiting . . . Godot, or the impossibility of the infinite present, says Yuri. I hope someday you will know how much I loved you.

Would Vima have become the renowned scientist she is today were it not for the Colonel? Or, should I say, had it not been for the Colonel? His devotion?" I have just typed the question mark at the end of chapter two when I am startled by the ringing of the telephone. It's the secretary from the Office. They need me. I have to be there in an hour at the latest. It's a pain, but I have no choice. I am under contract for the week. I'll be there. In an hour at the latest, she repeats. I confirm. Reassure her, irritated though I am. The book is just beginning to take shape. I find it hard to tear myself away from the computer screen. I switch it off, in a very bad temper.

The waiting room is packed. Straightaway I identify my compatriots among the men squeezed together on the dilapidated bench. There is just something in their gaze, you can't miss it . . . I go into the office and close the door behind me. The director, Mr. Hans, hands me two files and the day's agenda. He says, Students in graphic design, sentenced in absentia to fifteen years in prison. They were able to get out at the last minute. Three months spent crossing Central Asia until they got to the Schengen Area. Included in the file are copies of their caricatures representing the Commander as a fire-breathing dragon. Crime of lèse-majesté. Before you examine the files, Hans adds, read the insert on page 8 of the Posten, *the news-in-brief section. It's important. I open the newspaper. The title, in bold characters, makes my blood run cold. "Death by Drowning of Former Colonel from Theological Republic." I skip a few lines and focus on the end. The police have now ruled out the possibility of suicide voiced at the beginning of the investigation. According to the crime squad investigator, they are dealing with a contract killing, ordered from the country of origin of the former high-ranking officer, who was seeking asylum. I put the newspaper down on the table. Try to get hold of myself. It's freezing in here, I stammer, and I wonder if the heating hasn't broken down. I stand up. I rub my palms together. I hope the director hasn't noticed how my body is trembling. He says, This is the first case in series A. You know, the guy that the big boss questioned a few months ago. He asks, It was you who worked as his translator, wasn't it? I nod. I have difficulty speaking. Breathing. I go to the restroom. Lock myself in. Drink huge amounts of water. Splash my face. Anxiety is sawing through my guts. I take a tranquilizer. Wait for it to take effect before I go back to Hans. He says, One thing's for sure, the leader of that vile regime is behind this assassination. I don't care one way or the other if those guys go around killing each other, but for Christ's sake, why can't they wash their dirty laundry in their own country? I wonder why he didn't say "in your country." Does he really think I belong to his country now? He concludes, We have to be very vigilant. Pay close attention to the statements of the young men who are coming in today. Reread their depositions carefully. I nod. I pretend to concentrate on the files. I leaf through them, mechanically. Surprised by my silence, he eventually asks me what I think about the whole business. I shrug. Nothing. I don't think anything about it. And yet I would like to ask him why they did not offer him protection. And add, Aren't we also at fault, to some degree? Yes, I would say* we*—including myself in the Office—to pretend to belong. But I say nothing. I bite my tongue. He wouldn't understand. The* no *that is screaming inside me fills my lungs. Hans says no more about it. He calls in one of the two graphic design students. He is young, handsome, anxious. He sits down where the Colonel once sat. He spells his first and last* *name. Familiar sounds harmonizing so well with the echo of the* no *which persists all through the interview. The* no *which is burrowing deeper and deeper inside me. I listen, I translate, I transcribe. Like a robot. Just as I did with the Colonel. In this same room. After three hours of extreme tension I leave the place. Completely drained. Depressed. With this* no *throbbing, refusing to let go. The sky is low, the air is heavy. On the street corner I buy the evening papers and go into the first café I find in the shopping mall next to the building. The Colonel's death is not mentioned in any of the papers other than the* Posten, *which I have folded into my backpack. I drink my second coffee straight down, with a splash of brandy. I buy some running shoes in a sporting goods store. I run all the way home. There is nothing better than a marathon to deal with overexcited nerves.*

After a freezing shower I curl up in bed under the covers and read the insert in the Posten *at least a dozen times. Backwards, from bottom to top. Which gives: "drowning by murder . . . country our in asylum political requesting was." I would like to rid myself of words. The scandalous, inadmissible verb. Thus the act which is said to have occurred would be canceled out, given the absurdity and confusion of the statement. It's a subterfuge that takes me back to my early childhood. During those long winter nights when my grandmother was teaching me the secrets of the how the world was created from the mouth of the Goddess Atahina. By uttering the names of things she made them appear. She said* ocean. *Then* land. *Then* man. *And in that way she created the world and all the creatures that inhabit it. Do you understand, my little one? Then she wrote down everything she wanted to keep in this world. Tell me, Grandmother, if I write* ocean *and then erase it, will I make the ocean disappear? Try another word, rather. Take* cruelty, *for example. That will surely work. Then you will be allowed into the country of kind people. It's the nicest country in the world! Tell me, Grandmother, what word would you suggest today? Yield. Accept. Let go. Stop shouting* no. *Put an end to its vibrations, they'll drive you mad. There is no longer anything admirable about that sterile* no, *powerless in the face of what is irreversible. It's pitiful. Del won't ever be coming back. The Colonel is dead. He had warned me, after all. He knew, and so did I, that the men in power would eventually get him. For an assassin, even a reluctant one, there is no escape. And a traitor on top of it. I take a pill. Sleep. That's the only remedy. My nightmare is full of words. The words in the article:* drowning, murder, contract killers, agent, theological republic, asylum. *And other, older words. Those that are embedded in my soul. Words the goddess said, without my knowing it. Words that cannot be removed with the simple rubbing of an eraser.* Del, love, hope, reunite, abandon, betrayal, pain, nostalgia. *Words with sad or laughing eyes, terrified or indifferent. The Colonel's, Del's, my mother's, my father's. The glazed eyes of dead fish.*

I have been vegetating. For at least a week. Without a computer screen, a book, or a newspaper. I'm like a grub. It's impossible to work, to read, or to think. I run myself to exhaustion. I have to force myself back down to earth. I have to remember my promise. That's the best thing I can do for the late Colonel. Immerse myself in his life again. Bring his love back to life.

End of a new chapter. I take my finger from the keyboard. The telephone rings. There's a man, a certain Yuri, on the line. He introduces himself as a friend of Ala the Colonel. His English is as ragged as his voice, his Slavic accent. He wants to see me. It's urgent. The Colonel's name was Ala. I've just found this out. It's moving. I would like to know more. But I'm wary. This Yuri makes me uncomfortable. I ask, What is this regarding? And I immediately regret my words, I sound like some little bureaucrat. I'm not a secretary. I'm not someone who is particularly important. Fook, says Yuri on the other end of the line, not the least bit aggressive. And I repress my desire to laugh and say fuck, *and not* fook you too. *He says it again, Fook, don't tell me you didn't know they bumped off my buddy! Do you want to know more* about it or just fook it? I tell him to come to my house. He'll be here in an hour. He has the address.

Yuri is tall and thin. It's hard to tell how old he is. He has disheveled hair the color of wheat. Fluorescent green eyes of the sort to rip into a fainthearted soul. I have him sit down in the living area of my studio. I go to make some tea. Yuri doesn't move. Stares into space. I put the tray down on the coffee table. He takes a big, battered book from the inside pocket of his overcoat. Sets it down among the glasses and the teapot. He has no intention of moving it, that's obvious. I pour the tea. Too bad if his book gets splashed. He points to the title, in Cyrillic characters, and says, War and Peace. Tolstoy is my intellectual guide. And it is the first of the month. I wait. In silence. Somewhat taken aback. He asks, I don't suppose you have any vodka? All I have is cognac so I offer him some. It's okay, let's have cognac. Yuri insists heavily on his consonants. The C in cognac, or earlier, the K in his incomparable fuck, which he pronounces "fook," consonants grating on my ears. I point to the bottle on the shelf behind him. He reaches for it, shakes it gently, murmurs, This is what you call a drop. He empties the bottle, what was left of it, that is, into his glass of tea. He begins sipping his drink. He looks pleased. His gaze is sparkling. He has the eyes of a devil and an angel, half and half. Yuri picks up his book. Strokes it nonchalantly. He says, Every first day of the month I read a chapter from War and Peace. This edition dates from 1899, he adds solemnly. It's a treasure that will go with him until he dies. I am starting to lose my patience. I gulp down my tea all in one, and burn my palate. He notices that I am irritated. Be patient, I will explain. It is in this book that I found what I must leave with you. Ala was a clever guy. He knew all my habits. The rituals I never depart from. One month ago, when he left the envelope in the middle of the book, he knew I would find it this morning between eight and nine o'clock. And that's exactly what happened. I look at Yuri, my eyes open wide. He says, The envelope *contains two letters. One for me, the other for you. He hands me the two envelopes. I can keep both of them, he made photocopies. I grab them and shove them into the pocket of my trousers. My way of saying, You can go now, I want to be alone to read them. Yuri's gaze hovers, avoids mine, drifts aimlessly, Back and forth between the pocket of my trousers and the window. His way of replying to me, I understand, but I'm staying, I haven't finished yet. Yuri is the stubborn sort. I sink into the armchair. All right. I have time. I'm all ears. He begins talking. About the vital importance of rituals. The world has been based on rituals since time immemorial, he says. Whenever you have more than one two-footed creature, rituals will prosper. A detention center is no exception. The more lost a poor soul is, the more he will cling to his rituals. Everyone has their little obsessions. Ala had his. Yuri has his. They had a few together. Reading* War and Peace *in the 1899 edition, every first of the month, was a must—he pronounced it "moost"—for Yuri. For Ala, the must was his weekly pilgrimage to the planetarium. He went there as soon as it opened. And only came back out at closing time. Yuri tells me—in full knowledge of the facts—that the security people had trouble getting rid of him. He says, Twice I went with him. He was like a sleepwalker. He stared at the ceiling and the hemispheric screen, watching one projection after another. He didn't move. The guy was petrified, a real zombie, says Yuri. Wednesday evenings were devoted to their ceremony of tales from olden times and faraway places. Yuri was the moderator. He provided the vodka and embarked Ala with him upon his stories. He doesn't recall exactly when their nocturnal sessions began. Oh, it must have been one of those bluesy evenings when Ala asked him if he knew anything about stars. Yuri was a poet, after all. Yuri was astonished: he might be a poet, but no astronomer. Ala was so sad and disappointed he could cry. That's when the idea for the ballads was born.*

Yuri points to the empty cognac bottle and makes a face.

Nothing more to drink? he asks. Anything but tea. Something more substantial, he says. Would beer be substantial enough? Not really, but he'll make do, he has no choice.

I go and fetch two bottles of Eriksberg. No glasses. I like drinking straight from the bottle. So that's perfect. He does too, and not just beer. We laugh. We drink a toast. We relax. Yuri gulps down his first bottle of beer in one go. Ala couldn't understand why a poet didn't know anything about stars and galaxies! He got all worked up about it. To cheer him up before he started crying, I told him, that big dumbass, I've got something much better than stars. The Iliad *and* The Odyssey, *my friend. Who are they? he asked, the fool. I said, Concentrated humanity, plus gods, your fucking sky and all the rest along with it, you dumbass. And I set sail with him that very evening. Once upon a time . . . By the end of the week Ala was so hooked on Achilles that there was no way I— Yuri shook his empty bottle. I brought him another. I reassured him. My supply of beer is not inexhaustible but it is at least fairly substantial. Again he says, I don't know how many times I told him the story about Achilles. That's my whole tragedy, he would say. He made the story his own. He couldn't get enough of it. It had become a personal matter. Yuri looks at me, embarrassed. I suppose you've read— I nod before he finishes his sentence. Right, I may as well tell you, forget Ulysses or Oedipus or Phaedra. Not even Urania . . . I found out too late that his daughter was called Urania. I didn't even know he had a daughter. He told me when we were at the Imperial. At the restaurant. Ah, what an unforgettable evening. We stayed up all night long, would you believe. Fook, I miss the dumbass, says Yuri, despondently. A catch in his throat.*

I bring all the bottles I have. Eight in all. I line them up before him. He says that the evening at the Imperial should have gotten him thinking. In a disordered rush, he tells me everything that goes through his head while he empties the bottles one by one. He talks fast. Gets muddled. Gropes for words. Says fook *every other sentence—with words to fill in, hyphens, ellipses, exclamation marks, question marks—and then it's time for* fook *again. Most of his disjointed discourse is incomprehensible to me. An incoherent outpouring of sadness, regret, the refrain of I-couldn't-help-him, I-didn't-know-how-to-help-him, I-should-have-helped-him. He drinks the last sip from the last bottle of beer and says, Ala wore me out with his wife. First her ocher dress, then her golden gaze, then let's lay it on some more, and I'll finish off the bottle of vodka to the health of her intelligence. Are you trying to give me a hard-on or what, I would say, to calm him down. No way! Not even jealous, that dumbass Oriental. He just laughed. So I tuned out the rest. I didn't see it coming. I should have. I'd never seen him like that. I should have sensed bad luck was coming, with its underhanded tricks. He'd gone too soft for me to worry. And yet clearly he was saying goodbye. With a flourish. The real dumbass in the story was me. Fook, I'd never seen a man so in love. He was obsessed by only one thing, for his wife to be proud of him. Dead or alive. Looks like he's dead. For keeps. You know what you have to do now. Yuri jumps to his feet. The ball is in your court, he says, standing by the door, his big volume of* War and Peace *under his arm. Don't let this go unpunished. They killed him. They can stick their bull-shit human rights up their ass. Yuri rushes down the stairs as if the building were on fire. Without saying goodbye.*

I spend half an hour temporizing. Maybe it's time to scrape the blackened inside of the teapot? Or wash the windows? . . . I sit down at my desk at dusk. I open the letter addressed to Yuri first.

Fook, as you say, my friend. You see? They got me. You were right. The way you often are. They're a fierce bunch, the ones who call the tune. The ones who own the world. I say to hell with them now. I have nothing more to do with them. And I'm not dead yet. You'll only find this letter on the first day of next month. If I'm still in the land of the living you'll be able to tease me about it until the end of time. In the meanwhile, we're going to have a great evening together. That's the main thing. I'm so glad I met you, poet. Thank you for agreeing to have dinner with us. You'll see how beautiful she is, my Vima, in her ocher dress. I'm attaching a letter to this note. Read it carefully. Make a photocopy for yourself if you want to. As a memento. If I disappear, give the original to the person whose name and contact information you'll find in the usual hiding place. I know I can count on you to deliver it to her in person. As far as the rest goes, you can throw out a few of your best untimely fooks whenever you think of me. I'm going to look for Achilles. And you, old man, will have to wait for Godot. On your own. I'm sorry, I was beginning to like him!"

I'll read the second letter when I'm in bed. I'm going out to buy a bottle of cognac.

"Vima, by the time you receive this letter I will be dead. A few words regarding my great departure. My family must know. A few weeks after my last appointment at the Office, where you and I met, I had a couple of visits from the cops. Routine checks. So they claimed. Blatant lies, obviously. They were special agents from Intelligence. They questioned me as if it were no big deal. I made it clear to them that I was no fool. I made fun of them. Teased them. They didn't insist. There was no rush. We'll see you again, they said. They'd be back with good news! My situation should be settled soon. One week later they summoned me. To HQ. As if to say, We're not trying to outsmart you anymore, and we won't take you for a fool. This will be a meeting between equals. Between colleagues. The meeting lasted six hours. They were testing me. They wanted to know if I would be willing to collaborate with them. And if so, what was my price. What sort of collaboration? Consultant! Nothing scary about that. A cushy job that would consist of evaluating the psychological profiles of fanatical suicide bombers, how their terrorist networks function, how they are connected amongst themselves and with hazy organizations or states like the Theological Republic. After three months of training and an advanced computer course in a software that was new to me, I would finally obtain my papers. I would be able to send for my family at once. There was nothing dishonorable about the work. Vima would not object if I could talk to her about it. I would be on the right side of the fence. Against the dictators. I said okay. My job as a bookworm was not unpleasant. I had to go through files. Comment on them. Leave notes. Write up reports. Verify the authenticity of certain sources or documents. Decrypt secret codes, within the limits of my skills. But also, and above all, learn how to operate computer cameras and lasers remotely, as well as analyze weather data and maps of the terrain. It was all new to me and I found it really interesting. I was pretty sure, however, that this training had something to do with drones. The three months went by. Quickly. Smoothly. They congratulated me. They found me very gifted. But the papers they promised me were taking their time. They gave me one useless pretext after another. Gone was the atmosphere of trust. I left them in the lurch, and deserted their offices. We began playing hide and seek. One fine morning they called me. Summoned me. My papers were ready. I ran all the way. And there they were, on the desk, those damned papers. I felt them. Breathed them in. But I couldn't take them with me. Not yet. I had to do a mission for them. In a word, they asked me to do some more work for them. It had all been too good to be true . . . I reminded them of the terms of our agreement. My territory was the Internet. So I was determined to keep my ass on my chair. I refused to do any other missions. I didn't want to have anything to do with any sort of operation. I would not touch a weapon. Not even a cartridge. They said, You won't leave this office or your chair! And I told myself I'd been royally screwed. I waited for what came next, knowing perfectly well what it would be. They wanted me to go back to killing. To bomb targets by means of pilotless airplanes—drones, in other words. Planes which you could hardly see, but which sounded like thunder. I know something about it. I was on a mission in Yemen when American drones struck the village where a jihadi leader was hiding out, a guy they'd been looking for for years. He was killed along with a group of children who were playing near his hideaway. I remember the testimony of an American soldier who'd been a screen pilot for Predator drones, and after a few years of service he'd come down with PTSD. Anxious, insomniac, unable to communicate, disgusted with life. He was responsible for the death of two thousand people, including civilians, but also other American soldiers whom he had taken for the enemy. Collateral damage. The worst thing about it, confessed the soldier, was the disconnect between what seemed to be a game in an air-conditioned facility, and the violence wrought by his control buttons, causing death thousands of miles away! A soldier in war takes risks, and kills only the enemy on the battlefield. If all you are doing is killing on-screen, you lose all respect for life. I remember how sorry I felt for that Yank. Virtual war is a rich country's weapon, while the poor country resorts to terrorism. I abhor them both now. In the end I said to the director, I'm listening. He spread a map out on the table. The strike zone was on the border with our country. I was petrified. I asked them for some time to think about it.

That day I followed you along the waterfront I had reached the end of my deadline. What happened afterwards is of no importance. Except what you have to say to my wife. Tell her I kept my promises. Thank you.

"P.S. I have left clues in a secure electronic dropbox with proof that what I have said is true. My wife can have access to it if she so desires. She will receive the code at some point in the future. As for you, don't take any risks. Destroy this letter and forget everything. Above all, I do not want to cause you any problems. Be careful. The underground territory of Intelligence is often mined. No matter where you are."

I am dismayed. My thoughts are going round and round. Should I believe in a conspiracy theory? And why not believe? Because it is easier to point the finger of guilt at the Theological Republic. It suits me, and it makes sense. This is all beyond me. Why has the Office summoned me urgently in order to close the Colonel's file? He was not a priority. In his case I cannot suspect any of the zealous agents at the Office who, just before election time, wrap up all the outstanding files in order to empty the asylum centers of any potential job-seekers. It's the policy of ambitious civil servants toward political parties of every stripe. According to my colleagues, that is how the big boss obtained his position at the Office. But the Colonel could not be extradited. If the life of an asylum seeker, even a fascist one, is in danger in his country of origin, they hang onto him, even if they don't give him refugee status. So why would they have hurried the erstwhile officer's case, if not to force him to collaborate with the services in question? Did the big boss know about it? Or was it all done behind his back? Is that why they chose me as their translator? Another translator, in particular Professor Hilberg, the Colonel's usual translator, who is known for her unconditional empathy toward asylum seekers, would have noticed the slightest irregularity in his case. It gives me a cold sweat and, perhaps, some foolish ideas. Shouldn't I take the matter to the appropriate person? The press, for example? But what proof do I have to back it up? Should I talk about it with Lars? He would be thrilled at the idea of publishing a political document in the place of a personal novel. And Ala's wife? I can't do anything without her consent. She is still in the jaws of the lion. No, I can't do anything. Other than honor my promise and wait. I do decide, however, to suggest to Lars that we publish my manuscript in his "Life Testimony" collection. A compromise that is more faithful to the duty of memory, and which will enchant him, I'm sure. I fall asleep at dawn.

Nine months later, on a fine spring morning, Vima received a DHL parcel from the United States. The sender was the Colonel's wife. It was quite large, and contained a letter and a gift-wrapped cardboard box. Vima hesitated. Should she read the letter before opening the package or the other way around? For a long while she stared at the box, with its blue tissue paper wrapping, which was creased and torn in places. A web of purple ribbon was knotted in a tangled clump, stuck to the middle of the parcel with a heart-shaped sticker. She picked up the box, shook it, and put it back down on the table. It wasn't very heavy. She would read the letter first. She put it in her handbag and left the apartment. She needed human contact, people around her. She went to the most crowded outdoor café in town, ordered an espresso and opened the envelope. The letter was typed on letterhead from the Astrophysics Science Division at NASA.

Dear Vima,
In spite of all the precautions you took, I had to refuse to meet your contact. I didn't want to take any risks before leaving the country. He arranged to have the package re-sent through a traveler we could trust. Recently I received your letter, my husband's testament, and your manuscript. Thank you for your condolences. Before I reply to your request concerning your manuscript, and offer you my opinion in all sincerity, just a few words regarding my husband's

assassination. Thank you in advance for disregarding my language, which tends to be rather threadbare when it comes to feelings. When they were little my children reproached me for my mathematical way of speaking. They were imitating my husband. If human beings could communicate in mathematical language—which is more poetical than any other language—the world would be an easier place to live. Perhaps one day we will follow Nature's example, for her immense book is written in mathematical language, as Galileo has affirmed. But let us get back to the main thing. My husband's death was reported in the media and received a lot of commentary. It was a first, after many years. The policy of the regime—as you know—had hitherto consisted of silencing defections, particularly those of military personnel. But the murder of *that ignominious traitor* was justified as an *emanation of divine will.* This headline from an official newspaper typifies the tirades on the part of the pencil pushers in the service of the government, which has clearly claimed responsibility for the assassination. Henceforth one conclusion prevails: the leaders' change of tactics contains a clear message to anyone who might be tempted to follow Ala's example. They eliminated him and they'll start again. Anyone who might be bold enough to try now knows what to expect. Nowhere is safe. Like Ala's friends, I also believed he'd been the target of the despots. But now your letter, which refers to Ala's "testament as a free man," as he calls it, has stunned me. The news affected me above all because of my children, for they know nothing about the true circumstances surrounding their father's death. I'll tell you more when we meet, soon, I hope. I have been in the United States for not even two weeks. I just got my green card, and the administrative formalities regarding my employment at NASA are under way. As soon as my children are enrolled in high school and university, respectively, I will come and see you, if that's all right with you. I intend to bring a suit against persons unknown for the murder of my husband. The lawyer specializing in international law whom I consulted here suggested I sue the Theological Republic. In other words, to substantiate the theory put forward by the criminal investigation police in your adoptive country. According to the lawyer, that's the only way the mice will emerge from their hole. A situation that might seem comical if it weren't a tragedy for my children. Obviously I will be grateful to you if you agree to help me once I get there. Take time to consider any inconvenience or problems you might encounter before you decide. Don't take any risks. Regarding your writing, thank you again for taking the time to transcribe my husband's declarations so admirably. I recognize him, in the intensity of his emotions, but not in the way they are expressed, which is yours. His message is extremely important to me. My children will have to learn about it sooner or later. I am sure it will help them overcome the ordeal they are undergoing. They were deeply disturbed by the way the media went after their father. They could not wait to leave the country, despite their fear of the unknown and the sorrow of leaving family and friends. I'm sure they will be better off here than back there. Unless . . . There are always the what-ifs. Science is based on nothing other than what-ifs, and skepticism with regard to the preconceived notions that make up the material world.

Regarding the manuscript you hope to publish, you have asked me to give you permission to present it as the testimony to a life. If you insist, I have no objection. Even though as far as I'm concerned your book is still a novel. I read it as a novel. I did not see myself in your idealized protagonist, any more than I did in the relation with the husband. This relation has been sublimated, like all the characters. At the risk of disappointing you, I am far more ordinary—at least as an individual—than the Vima in the book. The scientist might eventually become admirable if she works at it. I haven't reached that point. Ala was blinded by his love. Would he have continued to be so blind if he had known and seen my shadow side? But then, how could he have, I hid it so well myself. We all do, to a degree, I think.

To try and help you understand me, I'll tell you briefly about myself. I was born into a lower-middle-class family. My mother was a teacher, my father an accountant. I was a studious child, I liked school, I worked hard, but no more than that. The discovery of my gift for mathematics dates from the time of my mother's death. I lost her when I was eight years old. I was raised by my father, who never remarried. He cherished me, protected me, and encouraged me. But gradually I withdrew into myself. A sort of autism, due to absence. But while I was turning into an introverted little girl, I also became increasingly curious. I made up for the lack of a mother through a quest for knowledge. I interrogated the sky, where my mother was supposed to have found eternal rest. I wanted to understand the world beyond my immediate surroundings, there on solid ground. I was obsessed by shapes and space, and naturally by figures and numbers. My professors could see I was brilliant at math. I was not much older than ten when, without knowing it, I happened upon the golden ratio. How did I do that? While playing. My games were solitary. I would draw shapes—squares, rectangles, triangles. I measured them, and constructed mathematical diagrams with the few tools I had at my disposal. The multiplication tables and a compass, basically. Purely by chance I discovered the so-called golden rectangle, whose side lengths are in the golden ratio. It was by juxtaposing rectangles of varying sizes hundreds of times that I obtained the visual result that was so surprising. I aligned two rectangles along their base, one horizontally, the other vertically. Then I drew a diagonal from the first rectangle and prolonged it into the second. Result: the diagonal line joined the tops of the two rectangles. I was in a trance. I tried the same thing again with certain rectangular books and it worked. I measured the sides of these rectangles and intuitively understood that it was the ratio between the two measurements that gave me this result. But I didn't know how or why. My father couldn't explain the miracle to me. He took me to see one of his friends who was a math teacher at the high school. It was a memorable day for me. The professor explained that this sort of rectangle is known as a golden rectangle because, indeed, the proportion between the long side and the short side of the rectangle is the same as that between the entire rectangle and its largest part. In other words, it is the golden ratio that makes a golden rectangle. To his great surprise, I understood everything he explained because I had already guessed it, even if I hadn't calculated it. He taught me how to do this: one plus the square root of five, divided by two. Everything became clear and a new world opened up to me. He had me take a test. At the end of this test he told my father, This little girl will go far. She's gifted, very gifted. Not long after that, thanks to this professor, to whom I owe my vocation, I was enrolled free of charge at the school for gifted children in the capital. I have wonderful memories of the two years I spent at that school. During the day I learned, and as soon as it was dark I studied the sky, playing with figures. I calculated the distances between the stars of the Big and Little Dippers with the help of a compass and some information I found in a science magazine. I was never wrong. My world fell apart when the revolution came. I had just turned fourteen. The school for gifted children closed its doors. My father was transferred to the provinces. He sank into depression, and the country was thrown into a state of unrest. Increasingly, I found refuge in the embrace of the Milky Way, while I waited for better days. And so I found out that the reason the galaxies seem to curl upon themselves like rose petals has to do with the golden ratio. I surpassed the level of all the instructors at the only school for girls in the little provincial town where we were living. They were all newly hired, on the basis of ideological criteria. My father was killing himself working as a taxi driver after his day at the office so that he could buy my books and pay for me to have private lessons. I became a true autodidact. That was the situation at the time I celebrated my fifteenth birthday. I had reached the level of the math baccalaureate, but I couldn't obtain it. I was expelled from high school, in spite of my grades—straight As in science—because I got an eliminatory F in ideological instruction. Naturally this F also disqualified me from the right to sit for the baccalaureate exam as an independent candidate.

This long preamble is to explain the circumstances in which I met Ala. I was desperate, but I hadn't given up. Already for some time I had been thinking that marriage might be a way out, although I scarcely believed it would. Of all my suitors, not a single one would have been any help. The help I wanted was to be able to go on studying. When I met Ala, I immediately knew that here was my chance. I didn't try to understand why I seemed to have so much power over him. But it was real, and completely different from the simple physical attraction which any man feels toward a desirable woman. How did I know that Ala would be the unconditional lover? It was more calculated than intuitive. From our first time alone together I knew I could get whatever I wanted from him. In addition to his physical attraction, another criterion which made him precious in my eyes was his future potential within the new regime. He was a soldier. He had been noticed at the front. He would be rising through the ranks fairly quickly. For me this was a guarantee of protection, and of the possibility that I might be able to go on with my studies under the best possible conditions. In a word, Ala and his position were the rampart I needed so badly if my projects were to succeed. There was no place in my life for the love with a capital "L" by which you set so much store. By the time I met Ala, calculating my probabilities where a predetermined life choice was concerned was more important than anything. Some people might qualify this behavior as purely cynical or opportunistic or who knows what else. Which would be wrong. As far as I am concerned, love—at least as it is understood by the great majority of individuals, and women in particular—should not have the vital importance that is granted to it. Given the choice, I would never have married and I would never have had any children. I would have dealt with my instincts by means of passing relationships. But such dreams were unthinkable, impossible, forbidden. In that country even more than anywhere else. A woman who dares to think such things leaves herself open to the worst consequences. I confess that if someone more interesting than Ala had come along, I would not have hesitated for a moment. But given the circumstances, I could not afford the luxury of letting this chance slip. One's vocation is founded on a projection into the future. Determination alone is not enough. The environment has to be favorable. I knew that at the first opportunity I was going to have to leave the country. With or without Ala. But I would proceed by stages. Ala never suspected a thing about my most secret intentions. Either before the marriage or afterwards. There was no point giving him any reason to worry. I had no intention of cheating on him, or abandoning him, or wronging him in any way. I let him love me. And I returned his love through my presence alone.

The heroine of your novel lives in a space-time of her own. You have done a very good job explaining how she manages to disregard everything going on around her, even though you justify it in an incredibly romantic way. My distance with regard to emotional outpourings is structural. My vocation is egocentric. I may seem inconceivably cold to people like yourself or Ala, who can burn like torches for love, for a cause, for an ideal. I have always rejected any feelings of belonging to a nation, a religion, a given place, or even a family. My homeland is science. When Ala used to talk to me so enthusiastically about defending the Fatherland, or the strength that faith can give, or his concern for the underprivileged, I wanted to burst out laughing. Like at the theater. But I held myself back. Regarding his work, as long as I needed access to the Army's observatory, I went along with it. I urged him to resign as soon as the conditions were ripe for us to leave and go abroad. The dissertation advisor for my doctorate by correspondence had assured me there was a position waiting for me. Ala knew nothing about any of this. But he suspected something. He knew me well enough to have an idea about my ambitions. Only abroad could I have a career. I think that unconsciously he was afraid of this. He thought I would slip away from him. He was right and wrong at the same time. I had always been slipping away from him, even though I was physically by his side. And there was no reason for that to change. Physically we got along well. There was good chemistry between us. Which is what drew me to him, above all. Other than that, I did not really pay much attention to what he was doing. I wasn't really interested. When he claimed that he had resigned, I was very happy indeed. So happy. The timing was perfect. We could leave. What could be easier for a businessman than to travel around as he pleased? I could never have imagined what actually lay behind his front of a job. I didn't have time to look into it any closer, even though a number of details, obvious clues, should have warned me that something was up. My own space-time, the silvery poetry of the heavens, occupied me entirely at that period in my life. I was preparing my doctoral dissertation. And the fact is, I trusted him. Now I know I was wearing a blindfold. Please forgive me for using this expression, but there is nothing innocent about it. I will get back to this.

My deep passion has always been and will remain astrophysics. No one, not even my children . . . could replace it. In short, my need for love to exist, to survive—in both senses of the term—has never had anything to do with Ala's. Instinct is in the DNA of all mammals. Of course I love my children. I will bring them up as best I can. But the love I feel for them is not a priority, nor is it in conflict with what constitutes the driving force of my life, the competitive spirit of research, a thirst for deciphering the fabulously complex phenomena of the universe. Orgasms in my case are above all cerebral. I will never understand women who talk about breast-feeding as the most supreme of pleasures. I hope that with these brutal confessions I will only disappoint the woman in you, and not the novelist. In your letter you confess to what transpires in your novel: your jealousy of the Colonel's wife, or rather, of the love she inspired in him. We do not inspire love, I don't believe that. Sometimes we elicit it when the other partner is in sync with us. Feelings are the result of a mental disposition. It is a strictly personal matter one keeps to oneself. Ala was afflicted by lovesickness. He had a visceral need to love beyond all bounds. The Commander, the Fatherland, his wife, his children, the underprivileged . . . He adulated them, and alternated between them, depending on the circumstances. I'm convinced he would have loved another woman with the same intensity if he and I had not met. He came upon me at the right moment. Happenstance. He needed to escape. I was his great escape. Indeed, I am convinced that love has no axiomatic reality. Which does not prevent me from telling you how much I admire your ability to love, to transcend. You surpassed yourself, you went beyond anything a human body can bear, in order to remain faithful to your concept of love. But this superhuman, or inhuman, challenge—is it not a matter for one's intimate self?

I am in your debt, and that is why I have been pressing the point where all this is concerned. I saved your life, and you rehabilitated me in my own eyes. I cannot find a better term to make myself clear. Now we are even. Thanks to you, I can accept my shadow side and my failings. I watched the CD several times, of *our* crimes toward you and so many other innocent people. I can say it without trembling, *our crimes*, even though, for years, I distanced myself from everything that I eventually reproached Ala with so violently. I was at odds with the situation and did not want to admit it. It was only after his departure that I had to face facts. Of the two of us, who was more to blame? The young devoted soldier caught in the tyrants' vise, or the scientist cloistered on her Olympus, refusing to see what was there before her eyes? An Olympus that Ala destroyed with a CD. The deep reason for my rage against my husband, which you render so well in your novel, is too shameful to admit. Why did he have to wrench me from my ivory tower just before we were due to depart? It was a question of his own survival. This constant need for an inconsolable love, a betrayed utopia. If I have an experience of soul-searching, it is something that I owe to you. It did not transform me. One can never change radically. But I won't lie to myself anymore, nor will I lie to my children. What is prodigiously human—not to say monstrously human—in Vima 455 cancels out the monstrosity, pure and simple, of the murderers at Heaven: that is a message I shall not forget. It is you I have to thank for enabling me to see what human beings can attain if they look inside themselves. I could never have imagined that a few inches of ground in the most sordid of prisons could elevate a person to the same degree as the constellations of the Milky Way. I have my work cut out for me, to meditate on my flaws and to reconsider the way in which all the world's believers are certain of a human purpose, something I have never paid any attention to before now, or very little. Science does not recognize either right or wrong. Before meeting you through that terrifying CD, I did not recognize any kind of truth other than the relative truth of science. Now, thanks to you, I can conceive of the complexity of the mystery of beings, the way that mystics experience it. Love is its axiom, and Utopia its motor. One day a poet friend told me that true meetings are merely instants, the fleeting magic which we call happiness, just to give meaning to the word.

Finally, as regards the parcel, it was handed to me at the airport. It is your husband's former lawyer who gave it to me. I took it. I trusted him. That's all I know about it. I will let you know as soon as I have the dates for my trip to Europe. You are in my thoughts, dear Vima, and I will see you soon.

Vima folds the sky blue silk veil, and places it next to the shoebox. Her hands begin to tremble when she sees the pair of little red boots in the box. A rolled sheet of paper, tied with a blue ribbon, is wedged between the boots. She picks it up, holding her breath. The poem that Del wrote to her years ago has been typed up and is followed by a sentence written in the hand of his eternal love.

The emotion is unbearable. She grabs the boots. Hurries down the stairs, barefoot, and enters the café on the corner of the wide boulevard. She orders a double cognac and drinks it in one go. The waiter who brings it to her hears her murmuring incomprehensibly. *"I miss you, one grows weary of an apple, of an orange, of life sometimes. I cannot do without them, your feet, they're so small, stamping the floor with anger. I ate my apple, drank from the orange, life goes on, when will you return, with your little feet?"* Vima recites her love poem, over and over.

The waiter brings her another cognac, and hears her saying to him, absently, *He's asking me to forgive him for not being here with me, and he's telling me he replaced the sandals with little boots to keep me warm, that's what he wrote. I should tell my namesake that love is the only axiomatic reality, the diagonal line to the divine ratio connecting kindred spirits. The mystery of our being is God's only refuge for when he feels like letting go.*

Her eyes brim with tears but they do not spill. The pale, barefoot woman squeezes a pair of little red boots to her heart, then puts them on and slips out the door.

About the Author

Fariba Hachtroudi decided to leave her home country following the Iranian Revolution in 1979. After relocating to Sri Lanka in 1981, she taught at the University of Colombo for two years and studied Teravada Buddhism. Hachtroudi then pursued journalism and eventually went on to write a full-length nonfiction account about her revisit to Iran after 30 years in exile called *The Twelfth Imam's a Woman?* In addition to writing, Hachtroudi also leads a foundation called MoHa for the advocacy of women's rights, education, and secularism.